beach body unknown

The Cherrystone Creek Mysteries: Book 3

Emma Jackson

Smith Beach Press

Editing by Debbie Maxwell Allen
Cover by Shayne Rutherford
Wicked Good Book Covers
Interior Design by Colleen Shannon
Ampersand Book Designs
Back Cover Copy by Shelley Ring

Smith Beach Press

HTTP://SMITHBEACHPRESS.COM

eBookISBN: 978-1-7338928-8-9
Paperback ISBN: 978-1-7338928-9-6

Preface

THE EASTERN SHORE of Virginia is a real place. A wonderful place. If you want to read some more about it, try AN EASTERN SHORE SKETCHBOOK by David Thatcher Wilson. Additionally, Cape Charles, Eastville, and Northampton County are real. Donna Bozza, mentioned in the book, is the Executive Director of the Citizens For A Better Eastern Shore, a group dedicated to saving the Eastern Shore from polluters, developers, and other n'er do wells. Yuk Yuk and Joe's is real, as are Machipongo Trading Company, Rayfield's, and Cape Charles Coffee House.

Most of the personal names in the book are amalgamations of the names of people from the Eastern Shore of Virginia (ESVA). I felt that using Shore-common surnames like Kellam, Smith, Goffigon, Heath, and others would add some verisimilitude to my story. They are not based on any real people, living or dead. Just borrowed the surnames.

Northampton County Sheriff's Department. Gentlemen, I do want to apologize for my characterizations of some of your people in this and my previous two books. I have the greatest respect for all law enforcement. I have absolutely no familiarity with any of your patrol persons or detectives. Don't know any of them. The negative stuff I've written about Detective Brooks (by the way, the name "Si Brooks" is actually from the former city manager of a North Carolina city, the late Cyrus Brooks) or senior deputy Pablo Gerena (a name fabricated by my computer's writing program) is pure fiction. I needed it for the story. So, forgive me, sheriff and deputies. I mean no harm nor besmirching.

Come Visit Our Website

Smith Beach Press

HTTP://SMITHBEACHPRESS.COM

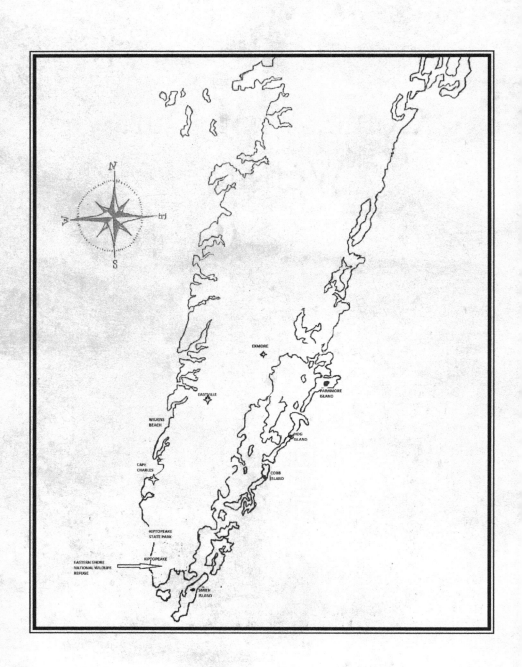

Prologue

THOUSANDS OF YEARS ago, the earth's climate changed, and the weather warmed, the mile-thick glaciers that had covered much of the planet began to melt. The glaciers retreated northward, leaving behind many major geological monuments, one of which was the Susquehanna River Valley. As the waters from the melting ice were gathered by the many small streams and rivers, they swept into the Susquehanna River and flowed south. The volume of the water was such that they overflowed the river's banks and spread over the land, from close to the Blue Ridge Mountains to the Atlantic Ocean. Eventually, these waters subsided, leaving rivers and streams and, most notably, the Chesapeake Bay. The Bay is a fairly shallow body of water, the deepest channel being the remains of the Susquehanna flowing deep down the center of the estuary.

Because of the shallow shelving nature of The Bay's bottom and the instability of the peninsular land of The Eastern Shore, it is no wonder that the severe winter storms that blow in fight to reclaim the alluvial land. Man tries hard to thwart the efforts of The Bay, erecting elaborate seawalls and groynes and jetties and dunes covered with sea oats. Still, each spring it is apparent that the winter has claimed more and more of the beach in The Bay's relentless efforts to join with its big sister, the Atlantic Ocean, just miles to the east.

The battle has continued since the Magotha, Mattawam, and Machapungo Indians first went to The Bay to harvest oysters and found trees that formerly stood high on the land now lying in the shallows, their roots washed from the earth by the surging waters. They recognized the subsidence of the land but did nothing to try to ameliorate it. Today, man's efforts have pretty much the same effect.

In modern times Cape Charles, near the southern end of Virginia's Eastern Shore, has become a resort town and views this loss of waterfront land with dismay. Beach loss equals revenue loss. The town had been originally founded by railroad interests who used it as a terminus where freight and passengers could be ferried across the Bay to Norfolk on the western shore. By 1884 Cape Charles was connected by steel rails all the way to New York and was a booming metropolis. It was never exactly big, but it was busy and prosperous ... until that is, the eighteen-mile long Chesapeake Bay Bridge-Tunnel opened in 1964, giving direct highway access across the Bay.

The opening of the Chesapeake Bay Bridge-Tunnel in 1964, and the widening of US 13, the Lankford Highway, the main artery on The Eastern Shore in 1965, rang the death knell for many small towns on The Shore that depended on the railroad and came close to killing Cape Charles. The town went into a serious decline until it was discovered by vacationers.

TOWN PREPS BEACH FOR SUMMER SEASON
By Wayne Creed
CAPE CHARLES MIRROR

It has been a harsh fall and winter for the Cape Charles beach. Several heavy storms have eaten away the sand and left tiny slivers around the parabolas created by the rocks.

When we talk about Cape Charles beach management, what we really mean is that the town basically does nothing. Since the channel dredging, the town has literally sat back and watched its prize asset dwindle away while pumping millions into the black hole of the harbor, and thousands more on sleazy downtown businesses.

The Public Works Director, the only real ally the beach has on the town staff, has finally taken some action to move some of the sand from dunes, and from the shallow part of the shoreline. At a glance, it appears the public works crew has doubled the available part of the beach.

Tensions between Public Works and dubious members of the Wetlands and Dune Board have run high regarding the beach. The Director told the Mirror, "Look, the beach is the top of the crown, it is the reason people come here. I tell my crew, that for the people that live here, and those that visit, when we do maintenance on the beach, do it in a way, a professional way, that makes it look like we care about it, and care about what we are doing."

The Wetland and Dune Board creating a beach management plan two years ago; however, critics have noted that it is really dune and shoreline management plan. In the past few years, that plan has worked, as the dunes got bigger, the shoreline closer, and the beach much smaller.

It was the Public Works crew, bulldozing part of the dunes down to fill in the beach, that uncovered him — a middle-aged male, tightly wrapped in heavy construction plastic and buried in the foot of one of the dunes.

One

THE MORNING WAS crisp and beautiful. It was just before dawn, and the coming sun was pinking the clouds with gorgeous shades of rose and mauve. The clouds lower down on the western horizon, over The Bay, were a deep vibrant purple. It was too early even for most of the birds to be awake, except for two ospreys soaring high over the water, looking for breakfast, and calling to each other.

James Nottingham Smith, or Nott for short, had left his shack before any light was showing in the sky and motored to the Cape Charles harbor. He tied off his scow and walked over to the beach to do his morning window shopping. That's what he called his beachcombing. There were lots of foreign ships, many of them colliers, anchored in The Bay in front of Cape Charles, and Nott liked to walk the early morning beach looking for any usable jetsam that might have washed up. That was how he furnished his shack up Cherrystone Creek, with flotsam and jetsam. Heck, even his scow was salvaged from the beach in the wilderness area just south of town.

He kept his eyes down as he walked. It used to be he'd keep his eyes down because his anxiety made him shun contact with others. But that was pretty much under control now, thanks to the efforts of Paige Reese. Now he kept his eyes down so he wouldn't miss any washed-up treasures.

He did look up in time to see a stately line of five brown pelicans slowly glide by. As he watched, he reflected on how unlike the high-soaring ospreys their flight was, but still how elegant and beautiful. Since almost losing his life in Iraq, then suffering from debilitating PTSD upon returning home, Nott was now savoring life — sucking out of daily commonplace things all the pleasure that was there.

As he walked, he heard the rumble of a Cat D4 dozer starting its cold diesel engine. He glanced over just as the Cat belched a plume of black smoke and waved to the operator. Nott didn't know the dozer operator's name, but virtually everyone in town knew Nott, and he was no longer viewed as a pariah. The town was proud of him as the local eccentric.

With a rattling diesel snort, the dozer began cutting into the dunes at the base and spreading the sand to widen the beach. Nott walked on. He'd finish scrounging this beach and then go to Rayfield's to visit Birdie and have some breakfast.

He noticed the sudden silence as the dozer shut down. He glanced back as the operator called to him. "Hey, Nott. Come look at this." He stood at the blade of his dozer, looking down at the sand.

"What'cha got?" asked Nott as he walked back.

The dozer operator looked white-faced. "L-l-look at this," he said as he pointed to the base of the blade. "I thought it was just some scrap plastic that had washed up. Then I saw that."

Nott looked and saw a long plastic-wrapped package … with a bare foot sticking through a hole torn in the plastic by the dozer. "Is that what I think it is?" he asked.

"I think it's a body," said the equipment operator.

"Oh, hell," said Nott. "Here we go again."

NOTT HUNKERED DOWN next to the package. It was indeed a body, tightly wrapped in Visqueen sheeting and tied with nylon crab pot rope. He touched the foot.

"Cold as a mother-in-law's smile," he said. "Definitely dead. Don't touch anything. We'll have to secure the area and notify the police. You got a cell phone?"

Nott dialed the dozer driver's phone, waiting as it rang. *Boy, Paige and Donna are going to give me a ration for not having that iPhone with me. Damn thing. Invades my privacy. Oh, well.*

"9-1-1, what is your emergency?"

Nott replied, "Cape Charles Police, please."

The call went through. "Sergeant Heath, please."

"Sergeant, this is Nott."

The police sergeant chuckled. "You're not who?"

"Sergeant, you're not Lou Costello, and this is Nott Smith. I'm down to the beach, and I've got another body."

TWO

ALTHOUGH IT IS rather presumptuous for man to think that he has any say in the matter, the National Audubon Society identifies four "flyways" in North America, which are used by migrating birds in the spring and the Fall as they chase moderate temperatures back and forth. The Atlantic Flyway starts in northern Canada and follows the east coasts of Canada and the United States south to the Caribbean and on to South America.

The Atlantic Flyway can be hundreds of miles wide, but in the Fall southern migration, many of the journeying birds hit the funnel that is the Delmarva Peninsula and are squeezed together between the Atlantic Ocean on the east and the Chesapeake Bay on the west until they concentrate at the tip of the peninsula in Virginia. Here they can "layover," finding food and protected resting places on the barrier islands and in the Eastern Shore Virginia National Wildlife Refuge's 1100 acres and in the 800-plus acres of the Kiptopeke State Park. Literally millions of birds — migrating songbirds, hawks, warblers, and even butterflies — converge here on their long journey south to rest and build up their strength to continue.

For over twenty-four years, the Eastern Shore Birding and Wildlife Festival based in Cape Charles celebrated this Fall migration. It drew an international crowd and featured a weekend of fellowship, seminars, boat trips and hikes, and a chance for avid birders to boast their knowledge to like-minded amateur ornithologists.

Although the organized festival is no more, the first weekend in October still draws people who want to see, in their wild habitats, bald eagles, peregrine falcons, red-wing blackbirds, brown pelicans, a variety of terns and gulls, and many more. They gather with their binoculars, picnic lunches, and warm clothes, sometimes greeting each other with the simulated high-pitched whistling chirp of the osprey.

It was just such a crisp October that found Paige Reese and Tim Hannegan picnicking at Eastern Shore National Wildlife Refuge. They had swung by the Cove Restaurant at Mallard Cove Marina to pick up some breakfast sandwiches and coffees for brunch, then gone to sit on the tailgate of Paige's REESE FUNERAL HOME pickup truck to eat, watch birds, and commune with friends doing the same.

"Do you think we should have brought Nott with us?" asked Paige. Nott was a friend of Tim and Paige, but still suffering a bit from PTSD due to an unfortunate incident with an improvised explosive device and an Army Hummer he was driving in Iraq. He now lived by himself in an Oyster Guard House on stilts in the middle of Cherrystone Creek.

"No," said Tim. "He likes to keep his own company. Besides, it's just too hard to get up with him. Even though Donna gave him an iPhone, he refuses to turn it on. Of course, he hasn't got electricity in that shack of his to keep it charged, either." Tim was a handsome FBI Special Agent whom Paige had been sort-of dating, neither of them too quick to make a commitment.

"I just don't want to give him a chance to relapse," said Paige. She snuggled down deeper into her cable-knit Irish fisherman's sweater.

"We'll borrow a boat and drop in on him after church on Sunday," replied Tim. "Okay?"

"I'd feel better," agreed Paige. "Maybe we can get him to go to dinner with us."

Tim nodded. His cheeks were ruddy from the cool October breeze.

As they sat there chatting and munching on crab, egg and croissant sandwiches, legs dangling over the tailgate, they were interrupted by Old Miss Mary. Old Miss Mary was a nonagenarian who looked as old as the crooked windswept trees perched on the tops of the dunes. She was a fixture in the Wildlife Refuge, living in a dilapidated shack of weathered-gray splintery boards that looked to have never seen a paintbrush. The decrepit hovel had been "grandfathered" in when the Refuge was established, expecting that the old lady would soon pass, and the shack could then be demolished. It hadn't happened yet.

Her abode had no amenities, and she got her water from jugs brought to her by her great-grandson, Edd, who kept tabs on her. They wouldn't let her use her outhouse anymore, so Edd had bought her a chemical toilet that he serviced every couple of days. Old Miss Mary said that she had been born a slave on Arlington, one of the plantations south of Cape Charles, but since very little notice was kept of black babies that many years ago, no one knew if that were so or not.

"Watchin' 'em burds, eh?" said Miss Mary. She was puffing on an old corncob pipe that smelled … well, it smelled like something had crawled up and died in her tobacco.

"Oh, hi, Miss Mary," said Paige.

"Mmm hmm."

"This is my friend, Tim, from across The Bay."

The old woman sized up Tim from the toes of his Topsiders to the FBI cap on his head. "Y'all dun't doff yer hat to an old lady?" she asked, eyeing him.

Tim snatched the cap from his head, nervously balling it up in both hands. "S-s-sorry, ma'am," he stuttered.

"Hmmph. 'At's better. Paige, you better larn 'im some mannuhs," she said.

"Can we offer you a bit to eat, Miss Mary?" asked Paige, smiling lovingly at the old woman.

"Naw," said the old woman. "Left my chewin' teef 'ta home. Wouldn't mind a bottle of cold watuh, though."

Tim broke the seal on a bottle and passed it down.

"Mmmph."

"Miss Mary's the last person living here in the Refuge," said Paige. "They grandfathered her in, expecting she'd pass on, and she fooled them and just keeps on keeping on. Right, Miss Mary?"

"Ayah," the old woman replied. "Ain't kickin' me outta ma home. Unh, unh. I fooled 'em good. I ain't gonna die 'til I'm ready. Ain't gonna give 'em the satisfaction nor you the bidness." She threw her head back and cackled long and loud as she walked away.

Tim shook his head. "Paige, I've said it before: you've got some real interesting characters over here."

Paige laughed.

Tim said, "Maybe we should get Miss Mary together with Nott. They could swap decorating ideas." Paige playfully punched him on the shoulder.

As they sat on the tailgate, some other residents of Cape Charles and its environs greeted them. Paige and Tim were now a well-known couple. But most just walked past, eyes to the skies, binoculars flopping around their necks, birds on their minds.

Tim crumpled his sandwich wrapper. "Paige, I love being with you. You know that. But ... what the heck are we doing here? We're not birders, are we?"

"No, Tim. Not officially. But I have to admit I do enjoy watching a lot of them. I love the way the pelicans glide so majestically just feet above the water and then land like a dropped bowling ball. And I love watching the ospreys hovering almost motionless way up there, then folding their wings and crashing down into the water, completely submerging themselves sometimes, and then struggling back into the air with a big fish in their talons."

Tim grinned. "Yeah, that's fun."

"My father's friend, Retha, was sitting on her steps at Smith Beach one day, just looking at the water, when an osprey flew over and dropped a big speckled trout right in her lap! My daddy used to spend hours out casting plugs on the flats at the mouth of Hungar's Creek, trying to catch a speck, and she gets a big 'un just gifted to her by a bird!"

Tim laughed appreciatively.

"Or I like just watching the sandpipers running back and forth trying to keep their feet dry while they probe the sand for food."

"Yeah, okay."

"But we aren't like these addicts who have their 'life lists' of species and are creeping around trying to spy out something new and strange. I did some research. There are some 10,000 species of birds, and some of these nuts set their whole life to spotting as many as possible. I read about one woman named Phoebe something who spent 18 years trying to see all 10,000 species all around the world."

"Did she do it?" asked Tim.

"No, she died 1500 species short of her goal. But, Lord, what an obsession. That's goin' just too far. Me, I just like watching birds. Like I just like watching sunsets."

"Okay. I get that. You — we — like watching birds do their thing. But why are we still here? We've watched the birds. We've eaten our picnic lunch. We've gotten enough sun."

"Yes, Tim, but remember — I'm a local businesswoman. I need to have people see me supporting our community. I have to maintain my good standing, or people are going to take their funeral business elsewhere. It's not like people are just dying to do business with me."

"Oh, ha, ha, ha. Okay. I get it. This is a business luncheon, then. Right?"

"More or less." Paige fashioned a pout. "Don't you just like being with me?"

Paige could tell from Tim's expression he knew she was teasing him. "Well ..." he said pensively and paused for effect.

"Tim!"

Laughing, Tim said, "Of course I want to be with you. Even if it's back out on that bird-poop covered breakwater ship, I want to be with you. Okay?"

It was Paige's turn to laugh.

Tim climbed down from the tailgate and stretched his back. Paige appreciated how, even with his jacket on, she could see his back muscles ripple and roll.

"But just how long does 'being with you' take in this wilderness?"

Paige looked around. "Well, things do seem to have thinned out. Let's get out of here. Maybe go over to Jackspots for a Bloody Mary before we head back up the road."

"Sounds great," said Tim, as they packed their gear back into the truck and headed out the road to the highway.

Three

IT WAS DÉJÀ vu all over again. Paige and Tim were sitting at a table on the outdoor patio at Jackspots, getting ready for their bloodies, when Paige's phone started vibrating on the table, demanding attention.

"Ignore it," said Tim.

"I can't," replied Paige. "Any more than you could ignore your cell phone. You know that."

Tim nodded, rueful and resigned.

Paige answered the call. "Miss Paige?"

"It's Sergeant Heath," she mouthed to Tim.

"Yes, this is Paige."

"Miss Paige, I'm afraid your boy Nott has found himself another body."

"Oh, for … where?"

"On the beach here in town."

"I'll be right there," she said. "Don't disturb the scene," and she hung up the phone.

Tim looked at her questioningly.

"I've got to go," she said. "Nott's got another dead body."

"I'm with you," said Tim.

Leaving payment and a large tip for the undrunk Bloody Marys, Tim and Paige headed up the road to Cape Charles in Paige's pickup truck. They didn't bother stopping at the police department but drove straight to the bayfront beach where they found cars from the Cape Charles Police Department, Northampton County Sheriff's Department, and the ambulance from the Cape Charles Rescue Service sitting, emergency lights flashing but, thankfully, sirens silent.

"Oh, Lord, I hope they haven't screwed up the crime scene this time," said Paige as they parked and jumped from her truck. She reached behind the front seat and pulled out a black nylon duffel bag. "My crime scene tools," she said in answer to Tim's questioning look.

They crossed over the dunes to the beach at one of the board overpasses and saw a gaggle of blue and green uniforms standing near a yellow bulldozer. Nott was there, too, so they hurried over.

Nott was wearing his usual canvas pants, faded flannel shirt, Army field coat, and filthy white rubber waterman's boots. His hair was tangled by the wind and in need of a trim.

"What's up?" Paige asked Nott.

Not saying anything, he waved his hand to the dune in front of the dozer.

Carefully walking around to the blade, Paige spotted a long package tightly wrapped in builder's plastic. "It's a body?" she asked.

"Yeah, there's a foot sticking out."

"Oh, yeah. Sergeant Heath," Paige called. "Why haven't you taped off the crime scene?"

"Oh, excuse me, madam coroner. We'll attend to that immediately. Is there anything else you would have me do … like maybe fetch you coffee and a cruller?"

Heath stood with his hands on his portly hips. The man knew that he should have protected the crime scene when he first got there, but it must chap his butt to have Paige point it out to him.

Paige ignored his sarcasm. She saw sheriff's detective Si Brooks standing in the crowd. "Detective Brooks," she called, "would you like me to assist in unwrapping the body?"

The nattily dressed detective hadn't intended to get down-and-dirty in the beach sand, but she had called his bluff. Homicide was the responsibility of the sheriff's department. "Yes, of course, Miss Reese. I would appreciate that."

Paige pulled on a pair of Nitrile gloves. Moving carefully so as not to disturb things too much, she used a pair of surgical shears from her bag to cut through the lines securing the plastic around the body. She carefully removed the ropes and placed them in a pile to the side to process later as evidence. Then she and Brooks began working on the plastic-wrapped body.

"Damn! The body's rolled up in this stuff," she said. "We can either roll it out of it or cut it off. What do you think, Si?"

"Well, harrumph, uh, I think … uh …" he replied.

"Yeah," said Paige. "I think so too. We should cut the plastic right up from the toes to the top of the head and then peel it back. I don't think spinning the body would be a great idea."

"Yes, of course," harrumphed the detective. Paige smiled at how easily she had been able to take control.

She took her shears and starting at the end where the foot stuck out, slit the heavy plastic sheet open like a cocoon. Unfortunately, this released a smell of putrescence, and Brooks, who had been hovering closely over the body watching Paige work, fell back gagging.

"Well, there he is," said Paige. "At least no animals worked on him."

"How long do you think he's been dead?" asked Sergeant Heath.

"No idea," answered Paige. "I'd guess a few days at the most. He stinks, but he's not falling apart, yet."

Brooks looked a little green. "Uh, Miss Reese, would you check his pockets for any identification?"

"Sure, Si. Just as soon as I photograph the body *in situ*."

"Yes, of course."

Reaching into her bag Paige produced a small Canon digital camera and proceeded to photograph the body and the scene from all angles. She took twice as many pictures as she needed just to keep the others standing around and reinforcing her authority.

After putting her camera back in her bag, Paige went back and hunkered down next to the body. She first examined the hands. "No rings," she said. "And he's not wearing a watch, although there is a tan line on his left wrist where one would have been." She tied small bags around the hands to protect any evidence that might be on them, like gunshot residue or anything under the fingernails.

"Paper bags?" questioned Brooks. "Isn't that a bit old school?"

"Not at all," responded Paige. "Plastic bags would allow moisture to gather and possibly spoil any evidence. And these aren't paper—they are Tyvek. They breathe, allowing moisture to escape while protecting evidence. Latest thing."

A disgruntled Brooks merely grunted.

"There's no pocket on his shirt."

The man was wearing khaki Dockers, and Paige gently slid her gloved hand into first one, then the other front pocket. "Nothing in his front pockets," she reported.

Carefully easing her hand under the body's butt, she felt in his hip pockets. "No wallet," said Paige. "And no chains or anything around his neck. The body's clean. No ID."

She looked up at Brooks. "You want to print him here, or wait until we get him back to my workroom?"

By now, the sun was high overhead, and even for an October, it was beginning to get warm out on the sand.

"Let's bag him, and I'll get his fingerprints when we've got him in your cooler," said the detective.

Paige looked at the ambulance crew. "Okay, boys. Tag 'im and bag 'im, and I'll meet you back at the funeral home in Eastville."

The ambulance crew took a rubberized body bag and stretched it on the ground next to the body. Then with one at the head and the other at the foot, they lifted the body with its plastic wrapping and slipped it into the bag. They zipped it closed, then used the straps on either end of the body bag to lift and place it in a stokes litter to carry it to their ambulance.

Once the body was gone, Paige knelt in the sand. She was glad she was wearing slacks against the cold as the coarse sand would have been uncomfortable on her knees. She gently ran her fingers comb-like through the sand where the body had lain, from one end of the depression to the other. "Nothing," she muttered, standing and brushing the clinging sand from her knees. "I'd hoped we might find something to help identify him."

Turning again to Brooks, she asked, "Doesn't the sheriff's department have metal detectors?"

"No," he responded, "but I think young deputy Holland has one." He chuckled disparagingly. "He likes to treasure hunt on his days off."

"Well, get him to bring it down here and scan this entire area," said Paige. "Maybe he can locate something that will help identify this poor guy."

Brooks pursed his lips, looking annoyed.

The sheriff's detective should have thought of that himself, thought Paige, and it must chafe him that a young girl like her was getting ahead of him, again. But his only choice was to comply or risk the investigation, and he knew that would hurt him even more.

"Yes, of course, Miss Reese," he muttered grudgingly.

"And Sergeant Heath, please keep the crime scene tape up until Deputy Holland can search the area."

"Yes, Miss Reese. Certainly, Miss Reese."

Paige knew that she wasn't making any friends with her perfunctory orders, but she couldn't worry about that. She had a body to deal with, and her professionalism insisted that all procedures be done by the book.

"Tim, did I forget anything?" Paige asked.

Tim smiled slightly. He'd seen this side of her before and knew that it was best to work with her and not rub her the wrong way. "No, I think that's got it."

"Nott?" she asked, glancing at the man standing quietly in the background.

"Huh?" he responded, seeming to come out of a trance.

"You've helped me before. Have I missed anything here?"

"No, ma'am," he muttered. "I just want to get shut of this place. Gives me the willies."

"You going to keep on with your 'window shopping'?" she asked.

"No, ma'am. I'm going back to my home where it's quiet. I've done found enough this morning and had enough excitement to carry me the rest of the month."

Paige smiled, and Tim clapped Nott on the shoulder as the man slouched back down the beach toward the city dock and his boat.

"Nott," Paige called. "Don't forget to stop by Rayfield's and get some breakfast."

But Nott just fluttered his hand up in the air in a noncommittal wave as he walked on with his head down.

Four

THE RESCUE SQUAD ambulance was waiting at the back door of the funeral home when Paige and Tim arrived in the Reese Funeral Home pickup truck. Tim had left his car at the Home when he arrived early that morning, so with a goodbye kiss, he headed south, back to his apartment on the western shore. Paige hated to see him go this early in the weekend, but she had a murdered man to deal with and knew she'd not be good for anything else this weekend.

Going through the front of the home to her workroom, she opened the back door for the ambulance crew. They were ready with the bagged body transferred to a stretcher, and they wheeled him in.

"Please put him on that end table," said Paige as she donned a mask, gloves, and a paper lab coat.

The men swung the body bag up onto the table, and Paige unzipped it. "If you want to wait for your bag you can just help lift him out onto the table." Once again, the two men grabbed the heavy plastic the body was wrapped in, and as they lifted, Paige pulled the body bag out from under.

"Hang on just a minute," she said. She took a powerful tactical flashlight and carefully searched the black plastic bag to ensure that nothing from the body was left behind.

"Nope, just sand," she said.

"Thanks, Paige," said the younger of the two as they took the body bag and exited through the back workroom door.

"Well, my friend," said Paige out loud to the corpse before her, "who are you, and how did you die?"

She carefully worked the plastic the body had been wrapped in down the length of the corpse until the unknown man was lying, still fully dressed, on the stainless-steel preparation table.

"Okay," she said, "let's try this again. Do you have any jewelry on? No. How about things in your pockets?"

Paige turned each pocket inside out into a plastic evidence bag. Nothing. Not even lint.

"Okay, my friend, you're going to be difficult, huh?"

Using her surgical shears, Paige gingerly cut away all the man's clothing until she was able to slide everything from beneath him, leaving him naked on the cold steel of the table.

"Bet you're glad you're dead, or that cold table would really shrivel you up," she said.

"What?" came a startled male voice.

Paige spun around to find Detective Si Brooks entering her workroom through the front door.

"Whew, you startled me," said Paige. "I thought that was the first time any of my clients actually answered me back."

"Umm, Miss Reese," said a somewhat embarrassed Brooks, "he's ... uh, nekkid." He looked away.

"I guess that's because I just cut all his clothes off. You'll want them for evidence, I'm sure," said Paige as she handed Brooks a large evidence bag containing the cut-off clothing.

"Oh, well, of course ... but must you leave him lying there? Like that? Aren't you ... embarrassed?"

Paige laughed. "I guess I was by the first hundred or so bodies I handled. Now, not so much. You bring your fingerprint gear?"

"Uh, yes," he muttered.

"Great," she responded, "let's roll a ten."

Slowly he repeated, "Roll — a — ten?"

"Yeah, Sherlock. A ten. A fingerprint card. Let's do it so I can get to work."

Together they managed to roll acceptable fingerprints for all ten digits. "Not bad," said Paige. "One time, Si, I had a body that had been in the sun so long that it was completely desiccated. I had to cut off the fingers and re-hydrate them before we could roll them."

"C-c-cut them off?"

"Yep. Just took my little shears, and POP! One portable finger. Toss it in some solution, let it plump up for a while, and voila — a printable digit. 'Course you had to keep track of which one was which."

Brooks started looking a bit green again.

Paige was having fun tormenting him. "If you've got to puke, do it in that sink over there," she said.

"Are you done with him?" asked Paige. Brooks nodded his head weakly.

"You want to watch for a while?"

Likely realizing his manhood was at stake, Brooks said, "Sure. I've got a little time. Of course, I've got to get back soon to scan these fingerprints and send them off to the databases."

Paige began her examination by turning on a huge overhead examination light and carefully going over the body inch-by-inch, looking for any anomalies. She had turned on a small recorder in her pocket. "No tattoos. No scars from incisions or accidents. No needle marks apparent on the arms." She moved down to the feet and examined between the toes. "No needle marks between the toes."

She examined the range of motion of his extremities. "No apparent broken bones." She looked at Brooks. "Of course, I'll check that more closely when I open him up. You going to stick around for that?"

Closing his eyes, Brooks gently shook his head as though it might fall off if he was any more vigorous.

She palpated the body's neck. "The hyoid bone feels as though it's intact." Looking again at Brooks, she said, "You know a broken hyoid is an indicator of strangulation." He nodded weakly. He seemed to be fading fast.

She took the man's head in both hands. "Oh! What have we here?" Paige rolled the man's head away from her and there, on the back of his head, was a contusion and a depressed fracture. "Is this what killed you, my friend?" she asked. "But why wasn't there a pool of blood in the plastic?"

Bringing the examination light down to where it brightly illuminated the gash, Paige gently probed with forceps while squinting through her Sherlock Holmes magnifying glass.

"Hmmm. Wood splinters," she said as she extracted a bit of wood from the wound. "Did someone smack you over the head with a Louisville Slugger or something?"

The corpse didn't answer.

"Look at this, Brooks," Paige said. "You can see splinters of bone with splinters of wood."

Brooks swayed a little on his feet and didn't look.

Positioning the man's head back upright, Paige pried up one eyelid after the other.

"Well, we might not have strangulation with a broken hyoid, but it looks as though we do have suffocation. Look. See the petechial hemorrhaging in the eyes?"

Brooks blanched and looked away.

"You can't see them as well with the death glazing, but it's there. That signifies suffocation."

Brooks was beginning to look like he wanted to be anywhere but here. Paige was enjoying his discomfort.

Leaving the eyes open, staring up at eternity, Paige frowned at the man's face. "What are these, acne?" she asked. Occasional little eruptions dotted the man's cheeks.

Paige levered his mouth open and looked inside. "What the heck?" The inside of the man's mouth was covered with little red holes, some of which had bled, but most of which just looked incredibly painful. "Is that some kind of sickness?"

Brooks quickly backed away. "I … I really gotta get back to the office," he said and hustled out the door.

Paige shrugged at Brooks' departure, grabbed her camera and began to take pictures of the wounds in the corpse's mouth. "What happened to you, my friend

AS SHE WORKED, Paige heard the crunch of heavy tires on the gravel of her driveway, followed by a polite knock at the back door. She opened it to find a Bob and Ray, a crew from the Northampton County Rescue Squad.

"Paige, sorry to bother you, but we've got a customer for you."

They wheeled in a stretcher with a body on it covered in a yellow plastic tarp.

"What do we have here?" she asked.

"A D.O.A.," Bob, the crew chief, replied. "So dead that the Staties didn't even bother running what's left of him up to the hospital."

"Oh?" said Paige.

"Yeah, he's an illegal who wasn't paying attention to where he was going. He drove full out into the back of a slow-moving farm truck, and since he wasn't wearing his seatbelt, he went straight through the windshield and ended up against the cab of the truck. He had so much crap in his car that he was obviously living in it. No I.D. Of course. The plate on his car was stolen, and the VIN came back, saying that the car was stolen too. So, they said to go ahead and process him as a John Doe, and after a period of time the county will pay to plant him in the back forty."

Paige opened the door to one of her coolers. She moved her brother Billy's case of beer out of the way. "Just slide him in here. I'll get to him, but I've got a more pressing case first."

"Yeah, we heard about that one. From down on the beach in Cape Charles?"

As the men struggled to transfer the body to the cooler, there came a sudden raucous "Aawrrk" from under the jacket of the senior man.

"Oh yeah," he said, "I forgot about this." He reached into his jacket and pulled out a small parrot.

"What's this?" asked Paige.

"Well, there's a problem with this here parrot," replied the ambulance driver.

"What's that?" she asked.

"Well, that's his owner in your cooler."

"And the problem?"

"Well, that's just it," said the man sidling toward the door. "Now he's your problem." And he quickly left, closing the door behind him.

"Wait a minute," called out Paige. "Wait! I can't take a parrot. I don't want him. I can't care for a parrot. And I've got a cat!"

Five

RALPH, THE PARROT, was perched on a gooseneck lamp on the desk in the workroom staring at Paige and bobbing just a little.

"What on earth am I supposed to do with you?" Paige asked him.

Ralph was an attractive fellow. His back was a vibrant green and he had a grayish-white bib that stretched down his front to his feet. He was about ten inches tall and sported a black leather harness with RALPH pressed into it. There was a short leash attached to a ring on the side of the harness, and Ralph seemed fine with just perching there staring at Paige.

Paige sat down on the desk chair and perused her new guest. "Damn it!" she exclaimed heatedly. "How the heck am I supposed to take care of you and an eighteen-pound Maine coon cat? When Pongo sees you he's going to think I've brought him a gourmet dinner."

Paige dialed her best friend. "Donna!"

"Paige, what's the matter? You sound frantic."

"What do you know about parrots?"

"WHAT?" Donna replied. "What are you talking about?"

"Have you ever kept a pet bird?" asked Paige.

"A what? Paige, what have you gotten yourself into now?"

"The rescue squad brought in a D.O.A. from the highway, and he had a parrot with him. They left the parrot and snuck off before I could stop them. What the heck am I going to do? I don't know anything about parrots!"

"What kind of parrot is it? One of those big red ones?"

"Donna, I don't know what kind it is. It's kind of small and green. And it's wearing a harness with the name Ralph on it."

"Ralph?" said Donna laughing. "Ralph?

"Donna, this is not a joke. What am I going to do with a parrot? If I take him home, Pongo will eat him. Damned big monster probably will just swallow him whole."

Paige grimaced. "Damn it, Donna, I don't need this right now."

As she sat there, the parrot looked at her, cocked his head, and said, very clearly, "Damn it!"

Over the phone, Donna said, "Who was that?"

"Donna," replied Paige, "that was Ralph! The parrot. He mimicked me!"

Donna laughed. "Paige, you're in trouble. You're going to have to watch what you say now." She continued with peals of laughter.

"D —, I mean, blast it!" said Paige. "Now what?"

"There's always the Internet," said Donna. "You don't even know what kind of a parrot Ralph is. Maybe he's valuable. Go research him."

"Well, I —"

"I'll bet you can even find training methods and how to care for him and everything. Give it a try and let me know," said Donna.

"Okay," responded Paige. "I'll talk to you later." She hung up the phone.

Paige took Ralph on her hand and went to her office. She let him climb up on her desk lamp and booted up her computer.

"Okay, bird. Let's see what variety of pest you are." She waited until her browser and search engine were running and typed in *Pet Parrot Breeds*.

Wonderful, she thought. *Pictures. This should be easy. Let's see. Parakeet? No. African Gray? No. Macaw? Thank goodness, no. They're huge! Cockatiels? No. Wait a minute ... Quaker parrot. That's it! Let me see: "long been prized for their charming personalities and talking ability."*

"So, little guy. You *were* talking to me. We're going to have to work on your vocabulary, though. I'll have to run down to Peach Street Books in Cape Charles and see if they have any books that can help."

She stood to leave her office. "Right now, though, I've got to get back to work. You want to stay here in the office?"

Ralph bobbed up and down a couple of times, then jumped to Paige's arm. He climbed her lab coat, across her shoulder, and settled snuggled up to the side of her neck.

"Okay," she laughed. "I guess you don't want to be left alone. Let's go."

Back in her workroom Paige continued processing the beach body. She was pretty confident that the cause of death was asphyxiation due to suffocation, so she carefully examined the mouth and nose for any bruising or foreign objects, such as threads if a pillow had been held over the victim's face. What she found was utterly unexpected — slime and a bit of seaweed. Dried eelgrass, to be specific.

"Where have you been dining?" asked Paige. She once again picked up her camera and recorded what she had found.

"Aawrrk," said Ralph from the desk.

"I don't know, Ralph. I'm not sure what to make of it."

It was getting late, and Paige was getting tired. She slid the body into the locking cooler she used for evidentiary bodies.

"Ralph," she said, "I'm beat. I've got to go to sleep, and I want to do it at my apartment, not upstairs here. But what am I going to do with you?"

She took his leash and let him hop back on her shoulder.

"How about I leave you in the bedroom upstairs for the night? Then tomorrow maybe I can figure something out."

Ralph just sat looking at her. It kind of unnerved her when she turned her head and found herself eye-to-eye with the bird.

Climbing the stairs to the apartment and going into the kitchen, Paige put a small saucer of water down on the table and eased Ralph off her shoulder. He went to the water and daintily drank.

"That's a good boy," said Paige. "Now, what can I get you to eat?"

She opened the refrigerator, but it was mostly empty. There was a Tupperware container of grapes, so she opened it and put it on the table.

This was more like it. Ralph quickly walked over, took one grape in his clawed foot, and began to nibble. Paige was ecstatic.

"All right! Tomorrow I'll do some more research about what you eat, but at least this should keep you for now."

As she started walking toward the door to the kitchen, a grape hit her squarely in the back of the head.

"Hey! What was that for?"

She walked back to the table and sat down, and Ralph calmly picked up another grape and began to nibble, all while eying Paige closely.

"I was just going to set a room up for you. Don't like to eat alone, huh? Okay. I'll wait."

Ralph ate a few more grapes then hopped back up on Paige's shoulder.

"The Internet said that you Quakers are very social. I can see what they mean. Have you adopted me into your flock?"

Paige walked down the passageway to the bathroom. "Look, Ralph, I'm not sure what kind of mess you can make, so I'm going to leave you in the bathroom. All right? I'll leave the light on, and I'll leave the water dripping in case you get thirsty. Then I'll be back first thing in the morning. Okay?"

Ralph just sat on her shoulder, bobbing his head up and down.

"Come on, now," she said. She unclipped his leash from his halter and set him down on the sink. "You going to be all right?" Ralph just looked at her. Paige eased out the door and gently closed it.

Suddenly a shriek issued from the bathroom as though a banshee had been trapped there with Saint Patrick. Paige rushed back in to find Ralph sitting in the same place on the sink. But in his eyes, she was sure she could see accusation.

"What?" she asked. "What do you want? I don't have a cage or anything for you. You'll just have to stay in here for tonight." Again, Ralph glared at her. "Okay?"

She exited again and eased the door shut.

SHRIEK! She burst back in. "WHAT?" she demanded. "What do you want out of my life? Damn it, bird."

"Damn it. Damn it," echoed Ralph. He tilted his head and glared.

"Okay," she said, reattaching his leash and putting him back on her shoulder. "Come with me."

She went back to her office and dialed the telephone.

A yawning Donna answered. "Yalow?"

"Donna, the damn bird won't let me leave it alone in the bathroom!"

"Damn it! Damn it!" said Ralph.

A smothered laugh from Donna. "Well, what do you want me to do?"

"I don't know," whined Paige, "but if I don't get home and get some sleep, I'll never be able to function in the morning. And I still have two bodies to process."

"And the bird won't let you leave?"

"No," she whined.

"What does he do, pout or something?"

"Oh, ha, ha, Donna. That's hilarious. No, he shrieks. Sounds like the steam whistle on the old locomotive. Like someone is tearing his wings off. And I can't take it, damn it."

"Damn it! Damn it!"

"Shut up, Ralph! Donna, what am I going to do?"

"Either you're going to have to stay the night there, or you're going to have to take him with you out to your apartment at the beach."

"But Pongo," cried Paige. "He'll eat him!"

"You're just going to have to keep the two of them apart. Pongo doesn't sleep on your bed with you, does he?"

"No, not usually."

"There you go. Ralph doesn't want to be left alone, and Pongo doesn't want to be with you, so just take the bird with you, slip him into your bedroom, feed Pongo some of that malodorous glop he loves, and get some sleep."

"Okay," said Paige. "I'll give it a try."

Paige was relieved to see how readily Ralph took to riding in the auto. "I guess you were living in the car with your previous owner, so this is no big deal."

It was a chilly evening, and Ralph snuggled inside the collar of Paige's jacket. "You're a real lover, aren't you?" she asked. It was kind of fun having an affectionate animal. Like most cats, Pongo was only attentive when he wanted something. The rest of the time, he seemed to consider Paige a necessary nuisance.

They arrived at Paige's apartment in about fifteen minutes. Ralph seemed to be asleep snuggled inside Paige's collar, so she was quiet, closing her car door and going into the apartment.

Inside, Pongo came up to her, loudly proclaiming that his dinner was late, and he demanded that she give him "the good stuff," and not some of that dried crap. Ralph had not stirred, so Paige went to the kitchen, opened a can of gourmet cat food, and dumped it on a plate for Pongo.

As Pongo ate, she unthinkingly took off her jacket and tossed it on a chair — with Ralph still asleep inside the collar.

"Aawrrk!"

Oops! Paige turned back to the chair but just as she did so Pongo, curious and called by the strange sound, came out of the kitchen.

"No, Pongo," yelled Paige.

Ralph extricated himself from the jacket and hopped up on the back of the chair.

Pongo looked up at Ralph and hunkered down, tail twitching fitfully. A low growl rumbled deep in his throat. His muscles tensed and bunched, preparing for his attack.

Looking down at the 18-pound cat, Ralph drew himself up ... and barked! Not a 10-inch parrot bark, but a 150-pound Rottweiler bark. A bark that said, "You're mine, pussy cat. Just wait right there." Again, the deep bark, followed by a convincing rumbling growl that was more threatening than Pongo's.

Pongo leaped to his tiptoes, glanced around frantically, and raced into the guest room where he cowered under the bed.

Ralph kept muttering in his Rottweiler voice while Paige just stood there, her mouth hanging open.

"Ralph, I — you — my goodness! I was afraid Pongo'd devour you. But … wow. I can't wait to tell Donna.

Six

EARLY THE NEXT morning, Nott was back on the beach at Cape Charles, searching for any salvageable items. The bulldozer was still sitting there but not running. Nott figured they were waiting until they were sure the crime scene was released. He remembered how furious and vocal Paige got when a crime scene was contaminated before being fully processed and figured the public works people didn't want to deal with that hornet's nest.

Down the beach, near the fishing pier, he saw an older couple walking the sands with a metal detector. He'd seen them out here before and on the beach at Kiptopeke State Park. They were locals who liked to search the beaches for anything lost by sunbathing tourists, and they'd been mildly successful finding occasional coins and earrings. They also found a remarkable collection of beer cans and other trash, so they always carried plastic shopping bags from Food Lion to dispose of the waste.

Although he was still quiet and withdrawn, Nott was trying to come out of his shell. He raised his hand to wave at the couple, but they never looked his way, concentrating instead on the sand at their feet. They were a funny older couple, probably in their late sixties. He was dressed in Bermuda shorts, sandals, and knee-high socks, and she always had on a homemade colorful big hat. As always, they walked side by side, not talking, him with earphones on swinging his metal detector tirelessly back and forth. She walked next to him, carrying what looked like a large split spoon for digging out their 'treasures.' Every few paces he'd stop and motion to the head of his detector. She'd move forward, hunker down and gently dig in the sand with her implement, then show him the beer can he'd detected before slipping it into her plastic bag as he continued his search with a oneness of mind.

This morning, however, her sifting produced something. "Papa," she shouted and motioned for him to remove his earphones. "Papa, look." Brushing away the sand, she held up a gold wristwatch.

"Mama," he exclaimed excitedly. "Look. It's a Rolex. And it's still running! Dig further. See if there is anything else."

Together they knelt and sifted through the sand, digging with their fingers. "Look!" cried the man. He held up an alligator skin wallet.

"Oh, Papa," she said. "Is there any money in it?"

"Oh my," he said, pulling out a bunch of one-hundred-dollar bills, then looking furtively around.

By this time Nott had walked up the beach to where they were. "Uh," he said. "That might be from the fellow got killed over there. We'd better call the police."

"No, indeed!" declared the man. "I know my rights. This is abandoned property, and I have salvage rights to it."

Nott was not into confrontation and backed off a little bit. "Well," he said, "I think we'd better let the police know. The body they found down the beach didn't have no identification. Police thought he'd been robbed, but this might be his stuff."

"You mean whoever killed him hid this stuff here so it would look like a robbery?" asked the woman.

"Could be," said Nott.

"No!" proclaimed the man. "This stuff was lost and abandoned, and it's rightfully mine for finding it."

"Papa, we don't want to get in the middle of a police investigation," said the woman. "Maybe we oughta do what this young man says and at least check with the city police."

The man grumbled. "Well, I ain't gonna call 'em. They show up while I'm still here, I'll show 'em what I got. They don't, it's mine."

This put Nott into a bit of a quandary. He still wasn't carrying the iPhone Donna had insisted on giving him. He knew where it was, back at his shack, but since he didn't have electricity, and since he wanted an excuse not to carry the intrusive thing, it wasn't even charged. He couldn't call the Cape Charles Police. This guy obviously wasn't going to. So, he'd have to walk to the police station. His legs were still somewhat crippled from his encounter with an improvised explosive device in Iraq, and it was painful for him to try to walk fast, but he set off with his hobbling walk to the station at the other end of town.

Fortunately, Sergeant Heath was at the station when Nott shuffled in breathing heavily. He explained the situation, and the two of them drove back to the beach, lights flashing but sparing the siren.

Crossing the dunes on the walkway near the cupola, Sergeant Heath walked directly up to the couple. "I understand you've found some evidence from my crime scene."

Still somewhat belligerent, the man said, "Well, I don't know about that. Me and my wife are just treasure hunting like we do every day. We didn't go anywhere near that area marked off with the yellow tape. We just stayed on our side of the beach. Mostly all we find is beer cans. Now and then we find a quarter."

"Once we found a silver dollar!" exclaimed the wife.

"What'd you find this morning?" asked Sergeant Heath.

"Oh, some beer cans and other trash."

"And …?"

"Well, we might of found an old watch."

"And …?"

"And … well … an old wallet."

"Any identification in the wallet?" asked the policeman.

"I don't rightly know," replied the man. "Never looked."

"Uh, huh. Where's the wallet now?"

"Well …" The man fidgeted. "Well, it's right here," and he reached into his pocket and produced the alligator-skin wallet.

"I thought you said it was just 'an old wallet,'" said Heath accusingly.

"Well ..." muttered the man.

Heath opened the wallet and pulled out the wad of one-hundred-dollar bills. "This why you didn't bother to look for identification?" he asked. "If you couldn't I.D. the owner then you couldn't return his money to him, right?" He counted the bills. "There's over $1,200 here. You were going to keep that? That's larceny."

He put the cash back in the wallet. "Here's a driver's license. You didn't look too hard at all, did you?" He read the driver's license. "Guy Coleman. Address in Pensacola, Florida. You know him, Nott?"

"Nossir."

"What else did you find?" demanded Sergeant Heath.

"Wa'll, just an old watch."

"Uh, huh. An old watch."

The man nodded.

"Let's see it."

"Well," said the man, "it was just an old watch buried in the sand. I've found 'em before. Ain't no big deal."

Heath held out his hand. Resignedly the man reached into his pocket and pulled out the wristwatch. He placed it in the policeman's hand.

"'Just an old watch'?" said Sergeant Heath.

The man nodded sheepishly.

"IT'S A DAMN ROLEX!" roared the sergeant. "And it's gold! With diamonds on the face!"

"Well, I thought they's just glass," said the man. "Up in New York, I've seen watches jest like that one selling on street corners for $25."

"So that's your story?" asked Heath. "An alligator wallet with over a thousand dollars in it and a counterfeit Rolex knock-off?"

"Well, you don't know," whined the man.

Sergeant Heath looked at him hard. "I think that you'd better get out of here before I charge you with grand larceny. And I don't ever want to see you on my beach again. DO YOU UNDERSTAND?"

"Uh, yessir," said the man. His wife stood next to him, head going up and down like a bobblehead doll.

As they hurried away, Sergeant Heath said, more to himself than anyone else, "What the heck is this world coming to?"

He turned to Nott. "Son, if you'll be so good as to watch this little patch while I go and get some crime scene tape and stakes, I'll drive you up to Rayfield's afterwards so you can get your breakfast. Okay?"

Nott nodded his agreement, and Heath went back to his car, returning in just a few minutes with the gear.

"Your buddy Miss Paige done got me real conscious of crime scenes, now. Don't want to ruffle her feathers. And I guess the sheriff needs to get his crew down here to sweep this area, now, too."

Nott nodded his agreement.

"Come on," said Heath. "I'll drive you up to Rayfield's. Got all the money in this wallet, maybe I'll treat you to breakfast, too."

Nott was horrified.

"No, boy, I'm kiddin'. Come on."

Sergeant Heath did stay with Nott for breakfast. As they were waiting for Birdie to fry up their eggs, he took the alligator skin wallet out and emptied it on the counter. "Driver's license—height and weight seem to match our body — credit cards in the same name, no photos or business cards. No receipts. Doesn't tell us much, does it? We've got a name now, but no idea what he was doing around here. Or how he got hisself killed."

"Nor how he got buried on the beach," said Nott.

"Asks about the same number of questions as it answers," said Heath. "Where do we go from here?"

Seven

NOTT KNEW WHERE he went from here. Once they had finished eating, and Sergeant Heath had gone back to the police station, Nott hitched a ride up the road to Eastville. The driver dropped him off across from the ShoreStop on Route 13, and he walked down Willow Oak Road to the Reese Funeral Home.

Nott had lived in the upstairs apartment at the Home, at one time, so he knew to walk straight through to Paige's workroom. As he swung open the workroom door, Paige yelled out, "Quick, close the door!" as a green-and-gray streak headed his way. The streak resolved itself into a parrot that landed on the lamp on the workroom desk.

"What the heck, Paige? You scared me half to death. Where'd the bird come from?"

"That's Ralph," she replied. "He came in with a D.O.A. from the highway, and now he's mine … I guess. At least for now."

"No kidding? What is he?"

"He's what they call a Quaker parrot. Supposedly they are talkers. Of course, so far he has only said one thing."

"What's that?"

"Well," said Paige, "it's kind of embarrassing. I was on the phone with Donna and was upset about getting stuck with Ralph ..."

"Ralph?"

"Yeah, the parrot. Anyway, I was kind of hot, and I said the 'd-word,' and the parrot said it right back at me."

"The 'd-word'?" questioned Nott.

"Yeah, you know. D-A-M-N."

"Oh! You mean damn," said Nott.

"Aawrkk, damn it. Damn it," said Ralph.

"Wow! That's pretty neat," exclaimed Nott.

"Maybe so here in the workroom," said Paige, "but can you imagine if I'm trying to arrange a funeral for some 80-year-old spinster and the blasted parrot starts swearing?"

Nott kind of laughed through his nose. Snorted.

"I just can't have that," complained Paige.

"How about just leaving him alone in here if you're working with a client out front?"

"Can't," said Paige. "He has separation anxiety."

"He has what?"

"Watch," said Paige as she took Nott by the hand and led him out of the workroom.

As soon as the door closed, there came an unearthly shriek from the workroom.

"Good Lord," said Nott. "What's that?"

"Ralph," was the one-word reply as Paige reentered the room. The parrot immediately calmed down and hopped onto her shoulder.

"I see what you mean," said Nott. "He does that any time you leave him alone?"

"Nott," Paige said, "can't you take him off my hands? You need someone to keep you company in that guardhouse of yours."

"No way, Paige. I value my privacy. And I'm not a pirate with a parrot on my shoulder."

"But he's only a bird," she said.

"Sorry," was his answer.

Ralph eased across her shoulder to where he could nestle in the warmth inside the collar of her jacket. "He doesn't much like the cold of the workroom," said Paige.

"What are you doing up here?" she asked. "Did Donna bring you up?"

"No, I hitched. I needed to talk to you."

He paused, and she looked at him expectantly.

"Some tourists found the dead guy's wallet and wristwatch buried on the beach."

"Near where the body was? I thought the sheriff's people went over that area."

"No, this was up near the fishing pier. They were sweeping with a metal detector and there it was."

"That's great," she enthused. "So now we know who our John Doe is?"

"Well," replied Nott, "we've got a name. Guy Coleman. But we don't know anything else about him."

"Hey," said Paige, "that's a start."

She walked over to the number one table. "Want to see him cleaned up?"

Nott had seen enough death in the war, so he didn't really care to see more, but he owed Paige a great deal, so he wanted to oblige her. He walked over to the table.

Paige pulled the covering down to the corpse's waist. "Here he is."

"How did he die?" Nott asked.

"Good question." She turned the body's head. "You can see where he took quite a blow to the back of his head, but that's not what killed him." Turning his head back upright she pulled up an eyelid. "Petechial hemorrhaging. He suffocated."

"Someone strangled him?" asked Nott.

"Not that I can tell. There's no bruising around the neck. His hyoid bone is fully intact. And there's no sign of someone putting a pillow over his face until he died. But I'll guaran-DAMN-tee you that it was suffocation."

"Aawrrk. Damn it! Damn it!"

"Ugh! I've got to watch my language around that blasted bird."

"So, what happened to him?"

"Nott, I wish I knew. Now that we have a name, maybe we can find out why he was in the area and where he's been staying and learn more from that. I'm going to clean him up a bit more and take a picture of his face that we can show around."

"Make sure you close his eyes," said Nott. "Those eyes would give people the heebie-jeebies."

Paige chuckled, nodding her head.

The front screen door of the funeral home slammed, and Paige sent Nott to see who it was.

Donna came in with two cafes con leche from Machipongo Trading Company. Her blonde hair was windblown, and her cheeks red. She'd obviously been driving with the windows open, enjoying the crispness of the air.

"Sorry, Nott. If I'd a known you were here I'd a brought you one, too."

"That's okay, Miss Donna. I had a full breakfast at Rayfield's this morning with Sergeant Heath."

Donna's eyebrows went up. "You and Sergeant Heath?"

"Yes ma'am. I was down on the beach when a couple of tourists found ... some stuff, and I went to report it to the sergeant."

"Stuff?" asked Donna, looking at Paige.

"Someone took the wallet and watch from our dead body and buried them elsewhere on the beach. I guess they wanted us to think it was a robbery gone wrong if the body was found without any valuables," said Paige.

"Anything interesting in the wallet?" queried Donna.

"No, just a Florida driver's license, credit cards in his name, and a little over $1,000 in cash."

"Nothing remarkable," said Donna.

"No, damn it," answered Paige.

"Aawrkk! Damn it! Damn it!" said Ralph.

"Oh," exclaimed Donna. "So, this is the bird you were telling me about."

"This is Ralph," said Paige. "Say 'hello,' Ralph."

"Hola! Hola!" squawked the little parrot.

"My gosh!" said Paige. "So, he does do more than just swear."

Seemingly on cue Ralph began to sing:

♪♪ *"Ay, ay, ay, ay,*
Canta y no llores,
Porque cantando se alegran,
cielito lindo, los corazones."

"Wow, Donna! He must like you a lot. He hasn't said anything for me but 'damn it.'"

"Damn it! Damn it!"

"Maybe you should take him home with you."

"Nice try, Paigey, but it won't work. He's yours. You make a nice couple." Donna smiled an evil smile.

"Oh! How'd it go with Pongo? How'd you keep him from eating Ralph?

"Donna, that was so funny. When Pongo saw Ralph, he started stalking him. He was hunkered down and his tail was twitching. I didn't think I'd be able to stop him. Then Ralph barked at him!"

Donna had been hanging her jacket on the back of the chair and whipped around.

"He what?"

"The parrot barked at the cat."

"Come on," said Nott, looking askance. "A barking bird?"

"Honestly, he sounded like one of those big — what do they call them — Rottweilers!"

"What did Pongo do?" asked Donna.

"He went up on his tiptoes like he'd stepped in something nasty and beat feet. He spent the night under the guest room bed!" laughed Paige.

"Well, that takes care of that problem," said Donna. "Now you don't have to choose between the two of them.

"But what about Tim? Has he met the wonderful barking bird?"

"Not yet. I haven't even had the time to warn him on the phone."

"Well," said Donna trying to stifle a laugh, "I hope the bird doesn't scare him off." She quickly held a napkin up to her mouth to control her mirth.

"Oh, very funny, Donna. Ha, ha. I thought you were my friend."

"I am your friend," protested Donna. "That's why I'm glad to see you've found a better companion than that surly cat." Donna sipped at her coffee. "I just hope your other companion likes him."

"Miss Paige, I'm sure he'll like him," said Nott. "Mr. Tim's a nice guy."

"Thanks, Nott. I guess we'll see."

Donna motioned to the draped body on the examination table. "Is that your latest guest, Paige?"

Paige admitted it was.

"Can I look? Maybe I've seen him around. I see lots of people through CBES."

"Sure, I guess so," said Paige. "I'm going to take a picture of his face to show around after I clean him up some. Don't suppose it's any kind of secret."

They walked to the table and Paige pulled back the covering from the man's face. "Look familiar?" she asked.

Donna looked at the face. "I'm not sure," she said slowly. "I may have seen him somewhere down in Cape Charles. What are those pinpricks on his face?"

"I don't know yet," said Paige. "Those are only the ones protruding through. Inside his mouth looks like the inside of a pincushion. Haven't figured out what they're from."

"How'd he die?"

"Suffocation," offered Nott. "Least that's what Paige said."

"Strangled?"

Paige looked at Nott to see if he was going to answer this one. When he didn't, she said, "No. No sign of ligature or manual strangulation. And no water in the lungs, so it wasn't drowning. Another mystery. I'll figure it out eventually."

Donna nodded, then looked at her watch. "It's getting on toward lunchtime," she said. "Want to call Pam and see if she wants to join us for lunch?"

"Sure," said Paige. "Give her a call while I clean up, and if she wants, we can stop at the post office and pick her up on the way to Yuk Yuk and Joe's. I'm sure she's going to want to find out all about my murder victim."

Donna chuckled. Pam Kellam, the postmistress, was also the prime purveyor of gossip in Eastville. "I'll go up front and give her a call."

"I'll be right there. You going to join us, Nott?"

Nott looked mildly uncomfortable. "No, ma'am, thank you. I think I'll just stay here. If that's okay."

Paige left Nott in the workroom and went out into the vestibule. She shrugged out of her lab coat to hang it on a peg when an aggravated "Aawrrk" issued from under the collar.

"Oh, Ralph! I forgot you were under there. Sorry."

"What are you going to do with him while we're out?" asked Donna.

"That's a problem," said Paige.

"How come?"

"Watch." Paige took Ralph and put him on the desk in her office. He stood there, bobbing slightly, watching her.

Quickly Paige slipped out and closed the door. A blood-curdling shriek came from the office.

Nott came racing from the workroom. "What's wrong?" he cried.

"Nothing," said Paige. "Watch." She opened the office door, and Ralph flew out and onto her shoulder, muttering as though cursing her under his breath.

"He is possessive!" said Nott.

"Now what?" asked Donna.

"Well," said Paige, "I guess he's going with us." She went back into her office for a moment and emerged with Ralph perched on her shoulder, wearing his leather harness with his leash attached.

"That'll do it," said Donna. "I'll drive. Don't want you distracted by Ralph blowing in your ear."

Eight

WHEN THEY PICKED up Pam, she was fascinated by Ralph and kept trying to get him to interact with her.

"Oh, my, what a pretty bird. Are you a pretty boy? Do you want to hop up on my finger? Kissy, kissy." She held out a finger. The nail was bitten to the quick and the tips were black with ink from sorting mail.

"Pam," said Paige, "you're making a fool of yourself. He's just a bird."

"Yes, I know, but he's so pretty." She switched to her baby-voice, "Isn't you, pretty boy?" She reached her hand over the seat toward Ralph, who promptly showed her that his beak was quite powerful.

"OW! He bit me!"

"Maybe he doesn't like baby-talk," said Donna, chuckling behind the wheel. "Did he draw blood?"

"Well, no," admitted Pam. "But it hurt!"

"He doesn't know you," said Paige. "For now, you'd better keep your hands to yourself."

"Donna," said Paige, "let's go on up to the Exmore Diner for lunch. I hear they've got a mess of soft crabs in, and I am dying for one of their soft crab BLTs."

"What're you gonna feed the bird?" asked Pam.

"Not sure yet. We'll see. Wonder if he'd like fried chicken or quail. You know, 'birds of a feather …'"

"Oh, Paige, that's awful!" exclaimed Donna, laughing.

The Exmore Diner was a throwback to an earlier time. Constructed in Patterson, New Jersey at the height of the diner craze in the fifties, its interior was still decorated with the yellow, pink and black tiles of that long-passed time. It only sat forty-four customers, in booths and at the counter, and was small enough that private conversations seldom were.

They sat in a black vinyl booth at the diner, and a waitress came to take their orders.

"Sweet tea all around," said Paige. The others nodded approval. "And soft crab BLTs."

"They come with Old Bay seasoned chips. Do you want any other sides?" asked the waitress.

While Pam and Donna shook their heads, Paige looked at the menu and said, "Yes. Would you bring one slice of tomato on a saucer, a very small amount of fruit salad, and the smallest baked sweet potato you have?"

"You want anything on the sweet potato? Butter or cinnamon?"

"No, just plain, thanks."

She looked at her friends on the other side of the table. "I'll give him a choice and see what interests him."

"Hey, Paige," started Pam. "What's with the murder victim from Cape Charles?"

"They just found a wallet, this morning, with a driver's license. Nott hitched all the way up to tell me. The victim's name is Guy Coleman. He's from Pensacola, Florida. But that's all we know so far."

"What was he doing on the beach?" asked Pam.

"Pam," said Paige patiently, "like I said, we don't know."

"Yes, but he must have had some reason for being on the beach," Pam insisted.

"Well," said Donna, "maybe he just laid down to take a nap, and the dune attacked and buried him."

"Oh, Donna," pouted Pam. "I was just wondering. Nothing much interesting happens around here, and when something does, well, I just want to know about it. You know — enjoy the excitement vi-vi- oh, what is that word?"

"Vicariously?" offered Donna.

"I know, Pammy," said Paige soothingly.

Their lunches came, and Paige looked like a glutton with all the saucers spread around her. She opened the sweet potato to let it cool. Then she took the tomato slice and cut it into small pieces. Finally, she spooned some of the fruit onto the saucer with the tomato.

Taking Ralph off her shoulder, Paige stood him on the table amid his feast.

Ralph looked around, bobbing his head, then tilting it to gaze at one of the saucers. With strange mincing steps, he walked to the saucer with the tomato and fruit. He delicately took a small piece of pear with one clawed foot and began to nibble.

"Whew," breathed Paige. "It said online that he'd eat just about any vegetable or fruit. I'll have to get him some unsalted nuts, too. We'll have to watch him at parties, though. No guacamole. Avocados are toxic to him."

"No kidding?" said Pam. She always enjoyed learning something new, even if it was virtually useless knowledge.

"So, Donna," said Paige. "You said that you might have seen my victim before. Any idea where?"

Donna chewed a bite of her sandwich while she thought. "No ... I'm not sure. It's just an impression, you know?"

Paige knew. But she hoped that Donna would remember something to give them a lead.

"Haven't been much of anywhere lately," Donna mused. "Wait a minute! I know. I saw him at the Cove Beach Bar down to Mallard Cove Marina. I remember because he got in a fight with another guy."

"Now we're getting somewhere," said Pam. "A suspect! Who was the other guy?"

Donna didn't reply right away. She glanced at Paige, then quickly averted her eyes.

"Who was he fighting with, Donna?" asked Paige.

"It was Billy. Your brother."

Paige sat in stunned silence. "Damn," she muttered under her breath.

"Aawrrk! Damn it! Damn it!" shouted Ralph loudly.

Suddenly everyone in the restaurant was looking their way. Paige tried to melt down into the cracked red vinyl seat of the booth. Pam looked mortified, and Donna tried to stifle a laugh behind her hand.

Paige grabbed Ralph and quickly tucked him inside her jacket. The warmth and darkness did the trick, and the fractious parrot quickly went quiet then fell asleep.

"That was interesting," said Donna.

"Donna, are you sure it was Billy who was fighting with the man?" asked Paige. "That puts him right at the top of the suspect list."

They discussed this new information and its possible ramifications all the way through their ice cream at the end of the meal. Then they walked outside and climbed into Donna's car.

"You don't think Billy could have killed the man, do you?" asked Pam with a quivering voice. She'd had a crush on Billy in high school.

"Lord, I don't know," said Paige. "Since he moved aboard his boat down at Mallard Cove, I haven't seen much of him. If he was drinking … or doing drugs … I just don't know. Damn it, Donna! Why Billy? Who else was down there? Anyone who might know what the fight was about?"

"I'll have Jim Baugh ask around. There's always a bunch of fishermen in there, and they just love to try to impress Jim with their tales, hoping he'll put them in one of his videos. He'll get them talking then see what comes out."

Jim Baugh was a local sportsman who made YouTube videos about fishing and promoted Cape Charles as a center for sports fishing on The Eastern Shore. He was gregarious, and it seemed he knew everyone.

"Thanks, Donna," said Pam, trying hard to stay in the middle of things.

Donna dropped Pam off at the post office, then drove up Willow Oak Road and dropped Paige at the funeral home. "Don't forget you've got your little buddy sleeping in your jacket," she said as Paige headed toward the door.

Inside, Paige carefully slipped Ralph out of her jacket and into one of the large side pockets on her lab coat. Then she hung up her jacket, donned her lab coat, and headed back to her workroom. As she went in, she shushed Nott before he said anything that would risk waking Ralph.

Knowing Nott's eating habits were far from regular, Paige had bought him a hamburger and fries before leaving Exmore Diner. They sat on either side of the workroom desk as Nott ate, and Paige told him about the latest news with Billy and the victim.

"Nott, I'm just beside myself. I can't ask Billy about it because it would just piss him off. But I have to tell Detective Brooks, or else I'm withholding what could be valuable evidence. But then he'll go interview Billy, and Billy will think that I sicced the law on him. So even if Billy doesn't have anything to do with the murder, he'll take offense at whatever I do, and it'll make the relationship between us more strained than it already is."

Nott just nodded his head, probably not knowing what to say or do.

"What'll I do?"

Nott shrugged.

Paige's cell phone vibrated in the pocket of her lab coat, waking a peacefully slumbering Ralph.

She first pulled Ralph from her pocket, depositing him on the desk lamp. "Que pasa?" demanded the parrot.

"That's a new one," said Paige as she recovered her phone. "Hello?" she said.

Ralph broke into raucous song,

> ♫♪ *"Ay, ay, ay, ay,*
> *Canta y no llores,*
> *Porque cantando se alegran,*
> *cielitolindo, los corazones."*

On the phone, a laughing Tim said, "I guess you still have the parrot ... unless Nott has started studying Spanish."

"Oh, Tim," she said. "I really need to talk with you."

"So, talk," he said.

"Can you come over for dinner at my apartment?" asked Paige.

"You sound distressed, Paige. What's up?"

"Just come over for dinner. We'll talk."

"Okay," he said. "I'll be there by seven."

"Thank you," she said and disconnected.

"Come on, Nott," said Paige. "I'll drive you back to Cape Charles. I need to go to Amy Nottingham's Seafood Market and see what I can get for dinner with Tim."

Putting Ralph back on her shoulder, they climbed into her car and drove south on Lankford Highway. Nott looked over as they passed Nottingham Seafood outside of Cheriton, but Paige kept driving until she deposited Nott by his boat at the Cape Charles town dock. Then she headed back to the seafood shop.

"What have you got that's good and fresh?"

The young girl working the counter was dressed in coveralls, a teeshirt, and the obligatory white rubber boots. She had a knit watch cap pulled down to try and control her mop of tawny hair.

"It's all good, and if it ain't frozen, it's so fresh it's probably still flapping."

"Okay," said Paige, "but I want something different. Not the same old flounder or trout."

"How 'bout swellin' toads?" asked the clerk.

"Blowfish? I've not seen a nice mess of them for years. You've got some fresh ones?"

"Yes, ma'am. Got us a few dozen 'sea squab' here that didn't get shipped north. You want 'em, I'll even clean 'em for ya."

"Done. Let me have half-a-dozen of 'em."

WHEN TIM SHOWED up at Paige's apartment for dinner, she was in the kitchen cooking. Ralph was perched in a proprietary fashion on her shoulder.

"Hey, Paige," said Tim as he walked into the kitchen to give her a quick kiss on the cheek. He leaned forward to give her a peck and was greatly surprised to receive a rather painful peck of his own—right on his ear.

"Ow!" he exclaimed, stepping back. Sitting on Paige's shoulder, Ralph bobbed his head as though inviting Tim to try to attack *his* Paige again.

Paige was laughing as she tried to mollify Tim. "I didn't realize he'd be quite so ... possessive. So jealous."

"Yeah, well, is that going to happen every time I try to kiss you?"

Amidst her laughing, Paige said, "I sure hope not. But, he's new to me, too. I don't know what he's thinking."

She looked at Tim with an impish grin. "Gee, I hope I don't have to choose between the two of you."

Tim did not see the humor.

At supper that night, Tim was impressed by the fried fillets of fish. Rather than the usual flat slabs with the occasional bone to watch out for, these were more like flaky rolls of delicious white meat with no bones to be found.

"This is delicious!" he said. "What kind of fish is it?"

Paige smiled. "At the fancy seafood houses in New York they call it 'sea squab.'"

"Well, squab's just a fancy way of saying 'pigeon,' so is this a play on words, too?"

"It's blowfish, Tim."

Tim stopped, fork in mid-air. "Blowfish? Isn't that poisonous?"

Paige smiled evilly. "A blowfish, or *fugu*, contains a poison that is 1,200 times more toxic than cyanide and has no known antidote."

Tim dropped his fork.

Paige laughed gaily. "This, however, is a species known as 'northern blowfish.' Not only is it not poisonous, but it is considered a delicacy."

"You're sure?" asked Tim, wavering.

Paige laughed again. "Got you, G-man. Yes, I've been eating these Chesapeake Bay blowfish all my life. They're great. The only bone is the spine, and there are no scales. You cut off the head, grab the meat inside with a pair of tongs, then just peel back the skin leaving two rolls of meat. I love them."

Tim kind of pushed the meat around on his plate with his fork.

"If you don't eat them, Pongo will."

He steeled his resolve. If they hadn't killed Paige, then he'd forget about what she said about the poison and just enjoy the fish. And that's what he did.

As they were cleaning up afterward, Tim asked, "So, tell me more about these northern blowfish."

"We used to think of them as trash fish and just threw them back. Then some Yankee came down for vacation and told us that they were actually good to eat. So, we started eating them. They're called blowfish or puffer fish or swelling toads."

"And you used to catch them?"

"Sure. They don't fight hardly at all. You just reel them in, unhook them, and toss them in the basket. Sometimes we'd turn one over and stroke his stomach. Then he'd suck in air and swell up like a little beach ball. As soon as you toss him in the basket or back in the water he'd breathe out and be nor-mal-sized again."

"Interesting," said Tim. "You'll have to take me out fishing sometime. Doesn't your brother own a fishing boat?"

Nine

"IT'S INTERESTING THAT you should bring Billy up. That's what I need to talk with you about."

Tim looked at her questioningly. "What's up?"

"Tim, I just don't know what to do." She filled him in on the alleged fight between Billy and the murdered man at the Cove Beach Bar.

"Are you sure it was Billy who fought with him?" asked Tim.

"I don't know yet. Donna is trying to get Jim to talk with some of the fishermen down there to see."

"How about what the fight was about?" asked Tim.

Paige grimaced. "I don't know that, either. We're trying to figure it all out."

"Did you ask Billy?" asked Tim.

Paige shook her head. "I guess … I guess I'm afraid to ask. I'm afraid of what the answer might be."

"Is this the kind of thing your brother might do?"

Paige frowned. "Oh, Tim, I don't know. Billy's never grown up. And he has a tendency to drink too much. But he's never been violent. He's always been kind of a … wuss. He'd rather avoid a fight if he can. He likes to say that he's a lover, not a fighter. Truth is, he's neither."

Tim said, "You know I don't have any jurisdiction in this case."

"I know," replied Paige. "But I thought you could give me some ideas before … well, before I have to turn my own brother in to the police."

Tim nodded his head grimly. "My best idea is for us to go down and confront him. I don't see any other way. It'll be a heck of a way for me to meet your brother."

Paige was visibly upset with tears making her eyes shine. Tim moved to comfort her. As he put his arm around her shoulders, he managed to dislodge Ralph, who had been perched on the shoulder away from him.

"Awwrkkk! Abandon ship! Earthquake! Attack!" A furious Ralph flew across the living area to his large cage in the corner. He ducked into its apparent safety and worked off his anger by loudly attacking the toys Paige had put in there for him. "Damn! Damn! Damn!" Paige quickly covered the cage, the darkness helping to quell Ralph's pique.

The next afternoon the three of them — Tim, Paige, and Ralph — drove south to the Mallard Cove Marina, where Billy Reese lived aboard his boat, an elderly black-hulled Owens Flagship Express Cruiser he named *Undertaker*. It was a stodgy old wooden cabin cruiser from 1959. One of the previous owners, who also owned a car dealership, had taken out the standard twin 220 horsepower Flagship Marine engines and replaced them with two 327 cubic inch Chevy small block engines. He'd called it the *Wild Rose,* after an old bootlegging boat. It was very fast but very fuel-thirsty.

"Permission to come aboard," called Tim from the dock next to *Undertaker.*

Billy was already well into his daily ration of too much beer and was sitting shirtless on a cheap plastic chair at the back of the boat. In deference to the sun, he had on a Tilley Paddler's hat and cheap mirrored sunglasses with Day-glo green monofilament fishing line as a retainer. Next to his chair was a chipped and dirty Styrofoam fish cooler, and empty Puddle Pirate Porter cans rolled around the deck as they stepped aboard.

"Well, baby sister," slurred Billy. "What brings you slumming down here on the docks?" Spotting Ralph perched on her shoulder, he added, "And when did you grow the second head?" He laughed beerily.

Motioning at Billy, Paige said, "Tim, this is Billy Reese, my *older* brother." She put a particularly disapproving accent on the '*older.*'

Billy was a beer-blurred mess. His long black hair was unkempt and hung greasily down to his shoulders. His cheeks and nose had the rosy glow that indicated either good health or, as in his case, capillaries burst from too much alcohol. He wore a torn and soiled Deadhead shirt, nondescript khaki fishing shorts, and filthy bare feet.

"Pleased to meet you, Billy," said Tim, proffering his hand.

Billy looked up at him blearily. "Who're you?"

Paige interjected. "Tim's just a friend of mine. He was with me when I decided to visit you, so I brought him along."

"Y'all want a beer?"

Paige answered for both of them. "No, thanks."

She sat one haunch on the rail of the boat. "Billy, I need to talk with you. Are you sober enough to handle that?"

"Something wrong at the business?" he asked.

"No, it's just ..." She paused. "Did you get in a fight up to the Bar a while back?"

Billy snorted. "I get in scuffles at the Bar all the time. Damn Yankees come down here with all their money, charter these big boats, and go out and catch all my fish. Sometimes I tell 'em what I think about 'em, and sometimes they ... take exception to it."

Paige took out a picture of Guy Coleman, and showed it to Billy. "How about this guy?"

"Man," slurred Billy. "He looks really bad."

"But did you get in a fight with him? A week or so ago?"

"Why?" he asked guardedly. "Did he press charges or something? He's lying if he did."

"Billy," said Paige patiently. "So, you did get in a fight with him?"

"What's he say?"

Tim broke in. "He didn't say anything, Billy. He's dead. Now, did you get in a fight with him?"

Billy looked up in surprise. "Who're you again? You the law?"

"Not in this matter," replied Tim. "I'm just trying to help your sister out."

Paige said, "Think, Billy. This is real important. Did you get in a fistfight with this man?"

Billy squirmed uncomfortably in his seat. "I don't know, Paige," he whined. "Maybe."

Tim jumped in. "Maybe? Maybe? Your sister is trying to keep you out of trouble, and the best you can do is 'Maybe?'"

Billy sniveled, "Well, you know if I had drunk a little too much beer ... heck, all them Yankees look alike to me. I don't know if he's one I fought." He turned to Paige, "I just don't know. I do know that I didn't kill nobody."

"Oh, Billy!" said Paige. "Listen to me ... I'm going to ask around up at the Cove Beach Bar to see if anyone else remembers. Meanwhile, you drink some coffee and sober up, and see if you can remember *if* you fought with him, and *why* you fought with him."

"Maybe I oughta jest get outta here," said Billy.

"You do that and it will look like you're guilty," said Tim. "Best thing for you to do is try to remember what happened."

"Billy, give me the keys to your boat."

"Paige! I ain't gonna do that. This is my home as well as my boat. I'm not letting you take her away from me."

"Billy, I just want to make sure you don't do anything stupid ... like run off."

"I won't, Paige. I promise," he whined. "Please don't take my boat."

"Billy, I'm going to have some of the other captains down here keep an eye on you. If you fire up *Undertaker,* they'll call me, and I'll have the Coast Guard run you down and bring you back in handcuffs. Understand?"

A cowed Billy nodded yes.

Back on shore, Tim and Paige wandered up to the Cove Beach Bar. It had gotten on to late afternoon, and the Beer-Thirty Bunch, a regular group of charter captains who met for brews and tall tales in the Captains' Lounge, had assembled. Paige wasn't a member of the group, but they all knew who she was, and she was welcome.

"Hey, Paige!" called captain "Baloney" Bill Cooper as she and Tim entered the lounge. "One of us dying that we don't yet know about?" Baloney laughed loud and long at his own joke.

"Hey, Captain Baloney. No, not that I know of. Besides, any of you salty dogs dies. I think we'll call the taxidermist, not the undertaker."

The assembly laughed.

Baloney Bill was a colorful middle-aged charter boat captain. He was loud, with such a heavy New Jersey accent he was almost incomprehensible to the locals. He was a key member of the "Beer Thirty" group of charter boat captains and was renowned for the ability to almost always have a beer in hand ... that he didn't buy.

"I do need your help, though," she said. She passed around the picture of the victim. "Anybody know this guy?"

The assembled captains and mates all looked at the picture, passing it from hand to hand.

"No," said Bill Cooper. "Don't look familiar to me. Any of you guys know him?" There was a general shaking of heads.

"Didja ask out to the bar?" he asked.

"No," replied Paige. "I thought I'd try you guys first. Well, thanks anyway. Captain Baloney, I owe you a beer." Everyone laughed.

They left the captains' lounge and went out to the public bar. Mimi Carter was tending. She was a stunning strawberry blonde in her early thirties who managed all the bars at the Marina.

"Paige Reese!" said Mimi. "You're down here pretty early. Have you turned pirate?"

"What?" asked Paige, confused.

"Is that a parrot on your shoulder?"

Paige took the time to introduce Ralph to Mimi.

"You want an olive, Ralph?" asked Mimi, and cemented a permanent friendship by providing the voracious parrot with a bunch of olives and maraschino cherries on a bar napkin.

"Now, Paige. You didn't come down here just to introduce me to Ralph. What can I do you for?"

Paige took out the photograph. "Mimi, have you seen this guy in here?"

Mimi looked at the picture. "Whew!" she said. "Boy looks worse for wear. I think he's spent too much time somewhere."

"He's dead," said Paige.

Mimi dropped the picture as though it had burned her fingers. "Dead?" she asked.

"They found him buried in a dune on the beach in Cape Charles. No one seems to know him, where he came from, where he's been staying or what he's doing here. Someone thought they'd seen him in here. Look familiar?"

Mimi gingerly picked the photograph back up and examined it.

"Yeah," she drawled slowly. "Maybe two weeks ago. Right?"

"You're telling us," said Tim.

"Who're you?" asked Mimi, smiling enticingly.

"This is Tim, my ... friend," said Paige. "He's helping me out."

Mimi nodded and returned to the picture. "Yeah. Now I remember. He was hitting on me about two weeks ago. Heck, I'm used to that. It's always happening. And mostly, the guys are harmless. But this guy, he was persistent, you know? I kept blowing him off. It was a busy night. Can't remember which one for sure. Then suddenly, Billy was there. Billy's been hitting on me forever, too, but he's pretty much harmless and usually pretty much fried. Billy grabbed the guy, spun him around, and launched a haymaker at his chin. Well, 'ol Billy was feelin' no pain, up to that point, and the guy easily ducked the punch. Then he planted one right in Billy's gut. You know, the solar pec ... solar ple ..."

"The solar plexus?" interjected Tim.

Mimi smiled at him. "Yeah, that's it—the solar plexus. Well, Billy went down like he'd been pole-axed. Jest lay on the floor, gasping like a grouper out of water. The guy just looked down at him, shook his head, and walked out."

"Did Billy follow him?" asked Paige.

"No, Billy couldn't even get up off the floor. Spuds and Murph finally picked him up and took him back to his boat. Billy warn't in no shape to follow nobody."

"Okay. Thanks, Mimi. And it was real nice meeting you," said Tim.

Mimi lit up with a thousand-watt smile. "It was real nice meetin' you, too," and she looked at Paige and gave her a meaningful wink.

Back outside, Paige said, "Let's get out of here and go over to Jackspots."

"Right," said Tim.

A short while later they were sitting on the outdoor patio at Jackspots. The sun had already set, and it was getting chilly, so Paige took Ralph and slipped him inside her jacket. Ralph loved the warmth, the dark, and the smell of Paige and promptly went to sleep.

"What do you think?" asked Paige.

"Personally or professionally?" answered Tim.

"Both."

"I think Billy's in trouble."

Paige nodded woefully.

"He claims to have no memory of the victim, he says that he doesn't remember the fight, yet we've got firsthand witnesses who saw him not only start an altercation but get whipped by the guy with just one blow."

Tim shook his head sadly. "Paige, I think you've got to give what you've got over to Detective Brooks."

"But, Tim, he's my brother!"

"I know that. But you now have pertinent information concerning the victim before he ended up dead. And it's not like it's a secret. Now that you've sparked the memory, once Detective Brooks gets around to questioning Mimi and the others, they'll be primed to finger Billy. And ..." he paused for emphasis, "they'll drop a dime on you, too. Brooks'll want to know what you knew and when you knew it. And if he wants to get pissy, he could accuse you of trying to cover things up to protect your brother."

Paige felt disconsolate. "Damn that brother of mine," she said.

A muffled, "Damn it! Damn it!" issued from inside her jacket.

Paige and Tim looked at each other and laughed, grateful for the minute of comic relief.

"Oh, Billy, Billy," lamented Paige. "What have you gotten yourself into this time?"

Ten

BACK ABOARD *UNDERTAKER,* Billy Reese wasn't sure what to do. One thing was certain — he'd definitely lost his buzz.

Billy was a boat bum, with all the negative connotations that encompassed. He didn't do any productive work, counting on Paige to keep the funeral business producing enough revenue for him to live in the manner to which he'd become accustomed.

With all the beer he could drink.

Billy's father, Big Bill Reese, had died of a stroke several years ago. Billy had been working with him in the Reese Funeral Home, but actually running the enterprise proved far beyond his meager administrative abilities. He resented the heck out of it, but that's when his little sister, Paige, came home from working on her MBA at The Wharton School to take over the family business.

At the time, Paige wasn't happy about the change either. All her life, she had wanted to escape what she saw as the provincial backwardness of The Eastern Shore. She saw her future as a powerful corporate chief financial officer in New York City. She knew, though, that if she didn't come home to save the family business, brother Billy would take it under and lose everything. So much to the chagrin of them both, Paige came back to run things and let Billy pretend to be the Chief Executive Officer, doing as little as possible.

As it turned out, Paige was successful beyond all expectations. Not only did she keep Reese Funeral Industries afloat, she managed to expand the business, diversifying into several related but separate areas. So successful was she that Billy was able to buy his boat and go live on it full-time, spending his waking hours in a pleasant beer-buzz, whether at the dock or out fishing. He liked to think of himself as a multitalented entrepreneurial sportsman along the lines of Jim Baugh but actually he was a pitiful drunk that everyone put up with, in memory of his well-loved and respected father.

It was this superficiality, however, that was causing Billy such trouble now. Everyone was happy to remember his arguments and belligerency and fights, but not so ready to give him the benefit of the doubt. Billy liked to say, "a friend will help you move; a real friend will help you move a body," then laugh long and loud. Now, however, friends were hard to find, and definitely not one who'd help with that body on Cape Charles Beach.

Billy's immediate impulse was to fire up the twin 327's and get out of there just as fast as he could. If he was careful, he could probably run down the coast and then over to Bimini or another of the Bahamian islands. There were so many out there, and many of them virtually deserted, he could maybe lose himself. He could repaint *Undertaker*, maybe change her name back to *Wild Rose*, and do some cosmetic work to her superstructure so she wouldn't be as recognizable.

Of course, he didn't have much money. But maybe he could get Paige to wire him money somewhere. She had to help him out, didn't she? He was her big brother and had always taken care of her. Of course, she would.

I know what I need to do. I need to get a legal pad and make a list. Billy's mind had trouble following straight paths of logic, so he had learned the trick of writing things down to guide him. He was an inveterate list maker. And his lists were pretty good. He'd think things through and get real detailed. Then, unfortunately, he'd decide that he needed a few more beers to clarify things in his own mind, or he'd decide that he really needed to 'sleep on it' for a while, and the list would be misplaced and forgotten. A tool is only as good as the workman who wields it.

So, Billy planned his escape. He made lists of the provisions he'd need for an extended cruise. He made lists of the maintenance he'd need to do, or have done, on *Undertaker* before heading off. He'd have to get the necessary nautical charts and lay out his cruise. Maybe he could talk that cute little bartender, Mimi, into going along. Offer her a cruise to the Bahamas. Girls love that kind of stuff.

All this planning was thirsty work, though. Billy thought that maybe another beer or two, more of that Cape Charles Brewery Puddle Pirate Porter, might help him think things out. Yeah, that was what he needed.

So, Billy went ashore and climbed the slight incline to the Cove Beach Bar. He was pretty sure the bartender would have pity on him, a regular, and sell him a six-pack … heck, maybe even a case … at a fair price.

Some hours later the bartender gently shook Billy awake. He'd been sleeping with his head down in a puddle of mingled drool and beer on one of the tables in The Captains' Lounge.

"Billy. Billy! We're closing. You've got to go back to your boat so's I can lock up."

Blearily Billy lurched to his feet. "Hey, thanks," he said. "Guess I must of dozed off. Been doing lots of work, you know."

The bartender helped him to the door, then pointed him in the general direction of the docks and *Undertaker*.

"Night, Billy!"

"Urrgghh," Billy replied as he stumbled down the hill and climbed aboard his boat. He collapsed, fully dressed, on the settee in the saloon. He never heard the torrential rainstorm that blew through, taking all his meticulously prepared lists and notes with it.

Eleven

IN THE MEANTIME, Sheriff's Detective Si Brooks had not been letting the grass grow under him. Once he had the victim's name and credit card, he had put in a request to the credit card company for a printout of his most recent expenditures. Gasoline, Hardee's, Watson's Hardware … wait, here it was. Apparently, Guy Coleman was staying at the Hotel Cape Charles.

Detective Brooks was not the brightest bulb in the chandelier, but he had been in law enforcement long enough that he was well-versed in protocols and bureaucracy. Rather than racing to Cape Charles and demanding the innkeeper give him immediate access to Coleman's room, he headed upstairs to the courtrooms to find a judge who would issue him a search warrant. With the evidence he had, that proved an easy task, and soon Brooks was headed south on the highway to the Hotel Cape Charles.

Detective Silas Brooks was a "come-here." He'd been born on the south side of Philadelphia and began his employment in law enforcement as a beat cop in Camden, NJ, home of Campbell's Soup. His career was lackadaisical, and he obviously had no future when he opted to bail out and go elsewhere, hopefully to somewhere that wouldn't check his bona fides too carefully. Fortunately, for Brooks, the Northampton County Sheriff's Department was in the market for a senior deputy after their serving senior had been killed while fleeing an arrest for human trafficking. Brooks might not have been a good cop, but he was skilled at padding a resume, and he was hired for the position. It was a low-pressure job, and just by showing up and suiting up, Brooks was quickly promoted to the office of Sheriff's Detective.

At the front desk of the hotel, he flipped open his badge wallet, expecting the gold badge to impress the innkeeper.

"Uh-huh," came the brusque comment. "Whadya want?"

"I'm Detective Brooks."

"Uh-huh."

"Uh, I need access to the room of one of your guests."

"Uh-huh." The innkeeper was less than impressed.

Brooks was getting furious. How dare this provincial putz treat him like this?

"You *will* escort me to the room of one Guy Coleman and unlock the room for me," said Brooks.

"Uh, huh," said the innkeeper, but just stood there staring at Brooks.

"Well?" demanded Brooks.

"Have you a search warrant?"

Oh, for Pete's sake. "Yes, of course I have," said Brooks as he took the papers out of an inner pocket and waved them at the innkeeper.

The man simply held out his hand, staring at Brooks.

"Why, you ..." But Brooks put the search warrant in the innkeeper's hand.

The innkeeper took his time taking his reading glasses out of a pocket. He held them up to the light to check them for smudges, then took out a handkerchief and gently polished first one lens, then the other. He slowly put on the glasses and began reading. Slowly. Nodding his head.

By now Brooks was seething.

"I retired as a defense attorney," explained the innkeeper. "I know you gotta read these things closely."

As the innkeeper read the warrant the door behind Brooks opened.

"Oh, hi, Nott!" said the innkeeper. "How can I help you today?"

"I was walking past, headed for the Coffee House, and saw Detective Brooks in here. I thought maybe it had something to do with that body I found on the beach, so I came in."

He turned to Brooks. "Does it, Detective?"

Brooks was close to apoplexy. Didn't anyone in this backwater have respect for a gold badge? He chose to ignore Nott.

After a moment the innkeeper looked up from the warrant. "You going to answer him?" he asked.

"IT'S NONE OF HIS CONCERN!" snapped the detective.

Mildly the innkeeper nodded his head and finished reading. "Well, it seems to be in order, Mr. Brooks."

"That's Detective Brooks," hissed Si.

"Oh, right. Well, then, *Detective* Brooks, if you'll join me, I'll escort you to the room of Guy Coleman." He looked at Nott to make sure he had received the message. "Nott, would you watch the desk for me while I escort *Detective* Brooks up to Guy Coleman's room so he can execute his search warrant?"

"Sure, long's you're quick I can cover it," he said. "But Detective, your face is looking awful purple. Are you sure you're okay? I can call the rescue squad."

The two men headed to the stairs.

"I suppose you think you're clever," muttered Detective Brooks.

"Hmmm?" answered the innkeeper mildly.

"Oh, come on," said Si, realizing he'd lost this battle.

The room was bright and airy, with a balcony overlooking Mason Street. It looked as though Coleman had planned on an extended stay as he had unpacked all his clothes into the dresser drawers and the hanging closet, stowing his suitcases in the closet.

Unlike Special Agent Tim, who believed in standing in the doorway before entering and letting the room "talk" to him, Detective Brooks pushed the innkeeper out of the way as soon as he had unlocked the door and bulled his way inside.

"You know," said the innkeeper, "you've a personality rivaled only by garden tools."

Furious, Brooks unceremoniously closed the door in the inn-keeper's face.

He returned to the lobby where he bid Nott goodbye.

Back up in Coleman's hotel room Detective Brooks just knew that he was going to find the critical piece of information to break open the case of the man's murder. He started by rummaging through dresser drawers. He expected to find ... well, he wasn't sure what he'd find. A gun? Gold coins? Maybe a dagger? Something probative. Nothing.

He went to the hanging clothes. He figured that he was more intelligent than the victim and carefully searched all the pockets. Nothing.

Brooks just stood for a minute, thinking. Then, having an "ah-hah" moment he dropped to his knees and started searching Coleman's shoes, pushing his probing fingers all the way up into the toes. Again, no joy.

Frustration mounting, Brooks moved his search to the bathroom. Taking Coleman's Dopp kit, he turned it upside down and emptied it into the sink. Nothing apparent. But Si Brooks was nobody's fool. He knew these nefarious types were talented. Taking the tube of toothpaste, Si squeezed it all out into the sink. Dipping the very tip of his pinky in the aqua-colored mess he carefully touched it to his tongue. Hmmm. Crest.

Not satisfied, Brooks took out his pocketknife and cut the tube open. Nothing. Then he took the full-sized bar of soap that had been in the kit and cut it in half. Well ... Irish Spring. Nothing more.

Getting desperate Si took the top off the toilet, hoping against hope that he'd find a tightly sealed packet of something. All he found was blue water.

What the heck? he thought. There's got to be something worth getting yourself murdered over.

Back out in the room Si cast around for something he could use. Then he saw it. Hidden behind one of the drapes to the outside balcony was a black aluminum Zero Haliburton brief-case. That had to be it!

Excited, Brooks took the briefcase and put it up on the desk. He paused, looking at its subdued elegance. His heart was beating hard. He reached out, put his thumb against the latch, and pushed. Locked!

Oh, for crying out loud. Now what am I going to do? There's gotta be good stuff in here if he left it locked! Arrrgggghhhh!

It was only a three-digit combination lock. The detective tried working the point of his knife blade into the lock to pry it open and snapped off the point of the blade.

He turned the briefcase over. Perhaps he could work on the hinges to get in. But, no, it was a well-constructed piano hinge with no sign of a gap where he could insert a tool.

Not wishing to destroy the attaché case, and possibly any-thing valuable in it, Brooks tucked the case under his arm and left the room. At the desk in the lobby, he gave a receipt for the attaché to the innkeeper.

"Find anything good?" asked the man pleasantly.

Brooks just spun on his heel and marched out the door.

Back in his office at the sheriff's department in Eastville, Brooks put the aluminum case in the middle of his desk. He turned on the overhead light and his desk lamp and closed and locked the door. He didn't want to be interrupted, and if he had trouble opening the case, he certainly didn't want to be seen struggling by the *hoi polloi*.

He started by just staring at the black attaché. Maybe it would psychically give him a hint. But the black metal case remained silent.

Okay, maybe I can squeeze a paperclip in there and slip the lock.

He fussed and fiddled, getting nowhere until there was a knock at the door.

"I don't want to be bothered," Brooks snapped.

"Uh, sir, that FBI agent and Miss Reese are here to see you."

Oh, crap! "Okay, bring them back."

Si examined the pair as they entered his office. *Damn Feeb, always trying to horn in on cases,* he thought. *And the girl! Who the heck gave her the authority to poke around in my investigations? She oughta be making babies or something.*

As they entered, Paige said, "I understand you searched Guy Coleman's room at the hotel."

"How'd you know that. The desk clerk tell you?"

"No," said Paige. "Nott did. And he said he saw you leave with a black metal attaché case. That it?"

"Yeah," said Brooks.

"What'd you find in it?" asked Paige.

Brooks was chagrined. "Nothing. It's locked. I can't get it open without destroying it, damn thing."

From inside Paige's jacket came a strident voice. "Awwrkk. Damn it! Damn it!" She reached into her coat and extracted the parrot, standing him on the desk. He shook himself a few times, then walked over to a case file placed squarely with OCD precision on the corner of the detective's desk … and pooped.

Brooks was livid. "What the hell?" he yelled. "That damn bird just soiled my case file."

Ralph responded, "Damn it! Damn it!" Bobbing his head up and down he glared at the detective.

"Sorry 'bout that," said Paige. "He gets excited."

"Do you want me to look at that attaché case?" offered Tim.

"What, do you have some fancy FBI voodoo that can get you inside?"

"No," Tim replied quietly. "Just training."

Shoving the briefcase across the desk Brooks grumbled, "Have at it."

Tim took the case and carefully examined the three wheels of the combination lock. "They make these pretty tight," he said.

Brooks sneered. "Too much for you?"

Tim just reached over and took the parrot-soiled page from the top of the case file. He reached in his pocket and pulled out a small Swiss Army Knife, opened the scissors, and cut a half-inch square from the corner of the paper.

Ignoring Brooks and looking at Paige he said, "Now watch this and learn something new, country girl."

He gently worked the ninety-degree corner of the paper down into the space next to the first combination wheel.

"You see," he explained, "there's a plastic disk attached to each wheel, and the disk has a slot in it. On a cheaper lock, we can push the combination wheel to the side and actually see the disk and rotate it until we see the slot. With better locks, like this one, we have to finesse it a bit."

He turned the wheel one careful click at a time. "What I'm doing is looking for that slot." He gently turned the wheel — click, click, click — until suddenly the paper slid further into the space next to the wheel. "There's our first slot," said Tim.

He moved on to the next wheel, inserted the corner of the paper, and repeated his turning of the wheel. Click, click, click, click. "There. Did you see the paper go into the slot? One more to go."

Tim progressed to the final wheel. Click, click, click. "There we are."

"Is it unlocked now?" asked Brooks.

"Not yet. But now we know that the slots are all aligned. So, we try the lock."

He put his thumb against the catch and pushed. Still locked.

"Didn't it work?" asked Brooks with a superior undertone to his voice.

Tim ignored him and advanced each of the three combination wheels forward one click. He tried the catch. Nothing. Once more he advanced each wheel forward one click, and this time when he pressed his thumb against the catch, the case popped open.

"Houdini!" enthused Paige.

"Awwrkkk!" said Ralph.

"Okay," grumbled Brooks. "You did it. Now let's see what's in the case."

Twelve

PAIGE HOVERED OVER the desk as Brooks carefully opened the case. This was his office, so she didn't dig in as much as she wanted to but just looked.

There didn't seem to be anything remarkable in the attaché, no weapons or stacks of banded currency, but there sure were a lot of official-looking papers. A small leather case held business cards, also. *Guy Coleman, Vice President of Site Acquisition, I-HAWK (IHAEC), PENSACOLA, FLORIDA.* The logo in the corner of the card was a hawk, wings spread, soaring in the sky. Brooks turned the card over. On the back was printed the ideograph, 热气

"What the heck is I-Hawk?" asked Paige. "And what are those squiggles?"

Neither of the men had any idea. They dug deeper into the papers in the case.

"Here it is," said Tim. "IHAEC, pronounced I-Hawk, stands for International Hot Air Energy Corporation. They're a wind energy firm."

"Wind energy?" asked Paige. "You mean like windmills?"

"Big honkin' windmills," replied Brooks.

"Then that explains this," said Tim as he pulled out a small hand-held anemometer.

"Well, what are they doing over here?" asked Paige. "I know some people are talking about putting a wind farm something like twenty-seven miles off Virginia Beach. But there's no place over here to put any."

Brooks said, "There is a lot of vacant land."

"But it wouldn't be economical," replied Paige. "Believe me, I studied finance at The Wharton School. If they are offshore, they have to pay some pretty hefty licensing fees, but if they tried to buy enough land on The Shore to put in a wind farm it'd cost them an arm and a leg."

"I sure don't know, Paige," said Brooks.

Tim kept digging through the documents in the case. "Feasibility studies, cost-benefit projections, land acquisition documents." He kept looking. "Whoa! What's this?" He pulled out a large sheaf of papers covered with ideographs.

"What is that?" asked Brooks. "Japanese?"

"Japanese or Chinese. I can't tell the difference," said Tim. "But I'd sure like to know what these say." Tim put the oriental documents aside and kept looking through the others.

"Here are some site diagrams. Paige, do you recognize any of these land shapes?" he asked.

Paige shook her head. "It's pretty rough. He sure wasn't a cartographer."

"Tell you what, Detective Brooks," said Tim in a conciliatory and professional tone. "How about letting me sign an evidence receipt for the briefcase and documents, and let me take it to my office? We've got an Asian special agent. I can never remember if he's Korean or Chinese or what, but maybe he can help us figure out what these documents say. If so, maybe that'll give us an idea of what Coleman was doing over here and who he might have pissed off enough to kill him."

"As long as you realize this is still my case. I'm not about to cede control of it over to you Feebies," said Brooks.

Tim tried not to take offense. "Of course not. It's not in our jurisdiction, anyway. I'm just offering a service to you."

"Uh, Detective Brooks," said Paige in a very subdued voice. "Uh … the reason we stopped by is that we might have a name of someone. Someone who got in a fistfight with Coleman down to Cove Beach Bar."

Brooks perked up considerably. He licked his thin lips as though preparing to taste something unusual.

"Well?" he said.

"Well," replied Paige, "we heard about Coleman drinking and hitting on the bartender at Cove Beach."

"Uh, huh."

"So Tim and I followed up to see what we could find out."

"You took it upon yourself to do this? Why didn't you report it to me?"

"I'm reporting it now," said Paige. "We were down at the Captain's Lounge they've got at Cove Beach, talking with a bunch of the charter captains … you know, showing them a picture of Coleman to see if anyone recognized him."

"Yeah, and?"

"No one in the Captain's Lounge recognized him from the picture."

"Are you going to get to some point with this dissertation, Paige?" demanded Brooks.

"I'm getting there. So we went out into the bar proper and talked with Mimi. You know Mimi? The manager there?"

"Yes, Paige. I know Mimi. What did she say? Did you show her the picture? Did she recognize Coleman?"

"At first she didn't recognize him. You know, pictures of a dead body can be hard to identify. Especially if it isn't someone you know well. And, of course, Mimi didn't —"

"Paige! Get to the point."

"I'm trying, but you keep interrupting." She made a sorrowful face.

"So Mimi said, 'yes,' she had seen the man before."

"And?"

Paige took a deep breath. "Mimi said that Coleman had been hitting on her and wouldn't take 'no' for an answer, and … and my brother, Billy … he lives on a boat there at the marina. Mallard Cove?"

"Paige!"

"Well, Billy was kind o drunk, and he came over and grabbed Coleman by the arm and sort of spun him away from Mimi."

"Okay, then what?"

Paige looked miserable. "Billy ... you know, he's not too bright but he does have a good heart ... well, he told Coleman to leave Mimi alone and took a swing at him."

"Okay, I got it. So Billy punched Coleman."

"Not exactly," whispered Paige miserably. "Coleman ducked Billy's punch then hit Billy in the solar plexus, knocking him to the floor. Then Coleman walked out."

"Do you think Billy followed him to get revenge?" asked Brooks.

"No! Billy was too drunk and too woozy from the blow. He just barely managed to get back to his boat. He couldn't have done anything. Not that night. But ... I just don't know if he did something later."

Detective Brooks stood, rubbing his hands together in anticipation. "Where did you say Billy was living?"

"He lives on his boat, *Undertaker*, in Mallard Cove Marina."

"Is he there now?"

"I couldn't begin to tell you. You'll just have to drive down there and find out for yourself," said Paige.

"I'm gonna do just that. Should I take a deputy along? Is he going to be violent, do you think?"

"I think he'll be more scared than anything. And probably drunk." She turned tear-filled eyes to Tim. "Tim, I can't go and watch Billy get arrested. He's going to know I turned him in, anyway. Would you mind driving down and making sure that everything goes allright? I don't want to see Billy hurt or anything."

"Sure, Paige," said Tim. "And then I'll come right back up here to be with you. If you want, I'll escort you to the jail once they've got him processed in."

"Yeah. That'd be nice of you," she said quietly.

"Let's go!" enthused Brooks. "We're burning daylight."

"Okay, John Wayne," said Tim. "But we're doing this by the book. There's no evidence that Billy committed murder or if he is violent. Don't get carried away."

"Heaven forbid!" said Brooks as he checked the load in his gun and slid his handcuffs into his belt in the back. "Let's go."

Oh, Billy, Billy, Billy, thought Paige as she watched them drive away. *Please be there on your boat and please, please don't do anything stupid and end up getting hurt. Dear Lord, I know that You protect fools. Please look after my brother. He's not much, but he's all I've got left.*

Crying softly, she walked to her car. As she climbed in, Ralph stuck his head out of her jacket and, as though mocking her, began crying in a loud, theatrical way.

"Awwrkk, bwa-hoo-hoo. Ay! O, madre!" He sobbed as though his heart was breaking. It was such a performance that Paige ended up laughing at him and affectionately stroking his glossy green head.

Thirteen

BILLY REESE WAS drinking beer in the Captain's Lounge of the Cove Beach Bar when Detective Brooks pulled up.

When Brooks and Tim entered the front of the bar and looked around, all they saw were tourists and some locals. They didn't see any of the charter fishing captains, and they didn't see Billy.

Walking to the bar where Mimi was tending, Brooks motioned her over.

"Hello, Detective Brooks," she said. "Beer?"

Brooks shook his head. "Seen Billy Reese?" he asked.

Involuntarily Mimi's gaze flitted to the doorway to the Captain's Lounge. He's in there swapping lies, and beers, with the Beer-Thirty Bunch. I imagine by this time he is feeling quite mellow.

Brooks turned toward the Lounge. "Uh, huh," he said as he started walking to the door.

"Please, Detective," said Mimi. "We don't want any trouble in here."

He sneered. "I won't be causing any trouble. I don't know about him. You want to call the po-leese?" he snarked. He turned and entered the Lounge. Mimi could only shake her head.

Detective Brooks stood in the door of the Lounge and looked around. The Lounge was crowded. It looked like most all the Beer-Thirty bunch were in attendance — Baloney Bill, Smitty, Shaker, Jimbo Morris — and many others. And there, ensconced amongst them, was Billy Reese, holding forth like a full-fledged charter boat captain.

"Billy Reese, Junior!" sounded forth Brooks in a deep commanding voice.

The room went quiet while everyone turned to look at the detective.

Billy, too far into his cups to recognize the sheriff's detective or Tim, responded, "That's my name. What's your game?" and collapsed in laughter. His companions, being marginally less muddled, tried to rein him in. "Billy, that's Detective Brooks. Chill out!" they whispered *sotto voce*.

Well on his way to becoming thoroughly comatose, Billy squinted at the detective and called out, "Brooks-y! C'mon over and have a beer. I'm buyin'."

"Wha'd he do, sir?" asked a well-lubricated Baloney Bill.

In his artificially deep cop-voice Brooks said, "Billy Reese, you're under arrest for suspicion of committing murder."

That lifted Billy slightly out of his buzz. "For what?" he exclaimed.

"Murder. Stand up and put your arms behind your back."

Billy slid his chair further away from Brooks. "Whoa, cowboy. Who'm I s'posed to have kilt?"

"I'm arresting you for the murder of Guy Coleman. Now, stand up and put your arms behind your back."

"Guy who? I don't know nobody by the name of Guy." Billy looked around at the men sitting with him. "Any y'all know a guy named Guy?" and he giggled at his witticism.

Opening his jacket to show the snub-nosed .38 in a holster on his belt, Brooks tried to sound severe. "Are you coming peacefully?"

"Shucks," said Billy. "Ah'm too drunk not to be peaceful," and again he giggled, looking around him for approval.

The others nodded in agreement. "You'd better go with him, Billy."

"But I don't know no Guy whatever. Who is he, Brooks?"

"He's the guy who knocked you on your butt a while back. Out in the bar. When you thought you were defending Mimi's honor? Way I see it, he knocked you on your butt and embarrassed you in front of the girl, so you lured him out into the Wildlife Refuge area and killed him to get even. Sound about right?"

Billy was starting to sober up more quickly now.

"Do you deny getting into a fight with him?"

Tim grabbed Brooks by the arm. "Don't you think you should Mirandize him first?"

Brooks yanked his arm away from Tim, giving him a vicious look.

"Well, we might have scuffled a little," said Billy, "but I didn't kill him."

Billy struggled up out of his chair. Detective Brooks spun him around and, while reciting Billy's rights, handcuffed him.

Beginning to panic, Billy looked around at the other men in the Captain's Lounge. "Ain't any y'all gonna help me here?" he whined.

"Ain't nuthin' we can do, Billy. You'd best just go along. Maybe Paige can help you figure something out once you're up to the jail in Eastville."

"But … but … I don't want to go to jail," exclaimed Billy, and he started to cry.

Hands cuffed behind his back, eyes bleary with tears, snot running from his nose, Billy was guided out the back door of the Lounge by Detective Brooks.

"I gotta lock my boat," Billy sniffled. "It's my home. I can't just walk off and leave it."

"Okay. Let's go," said Brooks as he guided the handcuffed Billy down to *Undertaker*, floating in its slip.

"How 'bout I go below and get some of my stuff … you know, toothbrush and such?"

"No way," said the detective.

"Well, at least take these handcuffs off so I can climb aboard and lock the main hatch," whined Billy.

Brooks stepped behind Billy and unlocked the handcuffs. Billy hopped down onto *Undertaker*, crossed the deck, and jumped into the water.

On the dock Brooks pulled his revolver from its holster. "Billy! What the heck do you think you're doing?" he yelled to the dog-paddling Billy.

"I ain't lettin' you take me to jail," bawled Billy as he started swimming away.

"You idiot! Just where do you think you're going to escape to? You gonna swim to Cuba?" hollered Detective Brooks.

Billy stopped swimming and started treading water. He looked frantically around him, as though a savior might swoop down in a helicopter and carry him to freedom, but all he spotted was a laughing gull. Who was laughing.

Billy turned and started swimming hard for the beach area of the resort. He kicked off his boots and britches and flailed away for all he was worth, which wasn't much. Detective Brooks simply walked down the dock and over to the sandy beach.

When Billy came ashore, he started to run away from Brooks.

The detective wasn't much of an athlete, but Billy was worse, and within ten yards Billy was face down on the sand, Brooks kneeling on his back, snapping the handcuffs back on.

He climbed off Billy's back and angrily yanked him to his feet, almost dislocating Billy's shoulder. He started to frog-march Billy toward the parking lot when Billy said, "What about my boat?"

"I don't care if it gets stolen or sinks at the dock. You had your chance."

"But ... but ... I'm soaking wet and covered in sand!"

"That's okay," said Brooks. "I'll spread plastic on the back seat so's you don't mess up my car."

"Yeah, but ... I'm wet. And the sand is getting everywhere. It's rubbing me something awful."

Brooks pulled Billy to a stop, turned him around, and put his face right up to Billy's nose. "You're lucky I don't strip you to your skin, turn a fire hose on you to sluice off that sand, and then throw you in the car stark nekkid. You don't shut up and I still might."

Billy swallowed hard, climbed meekly into the back seat of Brooks' car, and didn't say another word as they drove to Eastville and the county jail.

They issued Billy an orange jumpsuit to change into when they processed him into the lockup. Be begged for a shower to get rid of the sand and saltwater, but the deputies were less-than sympathetic after Brooks told them how Billy had gotten that way. Actually, they saw it as a just punishment for Billy's attempt to escape custody.

"You can have one phone call," Billy was told.

Still wet, still sandy, still miserable ... but no longer drunk ... Billy dialed the phone. He listened. One ring. Two rings. Three rings. Four ... Voice mail.

Billy looked at Tim. "Where the hell is she?"

Tim shrugged his shoulders.

"You got me into this, Paige! Now come and bail me out!" yelled Billy into the phone and slammed the receiver down.

Fourteen

PAIGE WAS BACK in her workroom. Since Tim wasn't coming over this evening, she decided she might just as well work. She pulled Guy Coleman back out of the secure cooler and was going over him again, making sure she hadn't missed anything important.

She was no longer talking as much to Guy, the body. She now had a partner with whom to discuss the case. Ralph perched on her shoulder. Due to the temperature of the work-room he snuggled close to her neck for warmth. When near the coolers, Ralph liked to get inside the collar of Paige's lab coat. Often he'd pull his head in and nap, but today just his head was sticking out, giving Paige a two-headed appearance. He'd cock his head as Paige talked to him, and sometimes he'd answer back or copy her. He was especially likely to do this when Paige lost her temper and used bad language. This was happening less often, however.

Maybe Ralph is good for me, thought Paige. *He's certainly helping me clean up my language. Daddy would be pleased.*

Paige could hear her phone ringing. She had left it in her office as she didn't want to answer it if her hands were covered in viscera. *It'll go to voice mail and I'll check it when I finish here,* she thought.

Ralph heard the phone ringing also. "Awwrkk, Ring! Ring! Phone!" he squawked.

"I know, Ralph. I hear it."

"Phone! Phone! Phone!"

"Shut up, Ralph! I hear it! I'll deal with it later!" Sometimes, thought Paige, it was like having a five-year-old hanging around. Ralph could be a real pain.

"Shut up! Shut up! *Cállate!*" said Ralph.

Just what I need, thought Paige, *a bi-lingual nag.*

With some difficulty, Paige rolled the body onto its side. "I want to look at that head wound again," she said to Ralph.

Fortunately, he had no comment.

"You see right here, Ralph? There's almost a vertical crease in the wound. Like someone hit him with something square-edged. And since it is vertical, and on the back of his head and not the top, whoever clocked him had to be shorter than him."

Ralph found this so fascinating that he pulled his head back inside the lab coat and went to sleep.

Paige kept talking to him, though. It helped her keep her clues straight. And she did have a small recorder going to back her up.

"You see, if it had been someone his own height or even taller the wound would have been higher up on the head if they had smashed down. It'd be higher, too, and horizontal if he'd been hit with a baseball bat swing."

She could feel Ralph moving around, getting comfortable.

"And it couldn't have been a baseball bat 'cause then the indentation would have been round instead of cornered like it is."

Ralph gave out what could only be thought of as a parrot sigh of contentment.

"Who hit you, my friend?" Paige asked.

Rolling the body onto his back and once again opening his mouth, Paige asked, "And what the heck are these?"

Pulling her examination light almost into the body's mouth and leaning in close with her magnifying glass, Paige again examined the numerous puncture wounds in Guy's mouth. This one had her stumped.

She was confident in her assessment that the blow to the head, while devastating, was not the fatal wound. It would have been disabling, but there was no doubt in her mind that the final demise was due to asphyxiation. But she was equally certain that there was no manual or ligature strangulation because there simply were no signs of it.

"How'd they do it?" Paige asked. "There's no bruising from anything being pushed over your face, like a pillow. There's no sign of threads or anything from a cloth being shoved down your throat. How'd they do it?"

The body just lay there.

Paige started violently as a loud, "How'd? How'd?" issued from under her lab coat. She had forgotten Ralph was asleep in there.

"Okay, Ralph, what do you think? We've got to figure this out."

Ralph climbed back out, shook himself, bobbed his head while looking at Paige, and promptly pooped on her lab coat.

"All right. I guess I deserved that for waking you up.

"You ready for dinner?"

Paige took off her soiled lab coat and tossed it in the laundry on her way to her office. It was already dark outside, and she had to feel her way to the light switch. As she reached for the switch, she saw the LEDs blinking on her cell phone and remembered the phone call she had ignored.

Curious as to who had called, Paige unlocked her phone. The missed call phone number and identification displayed on the top screen. "Northampton County Sheriff."

Oh, dear. I wonder what that's about.

If it had been a body they would have brought it to her back door. *Maybe they found out something about Guy Coleman,* she thought.

She dialed the voice mail and listened. "YOU GOT ME INTO THIS, PAIGE! NOW COME AND BAIL ME OUT!" Billy.

Paige closed her eyes and sighed.

I guess Deputy Dawg must have acted on that tip I gave him, she thought. *Oh, this is going to be fun.*

Uncertain of how the sheriff's department was going to react to Ralph, she tucked him inside her jacket, where, in the warmth and dark, he immediately fell asleep. Then she drove the quarter-mile to the jail.

Being rather strong-willed … or hot-headed, if you'd rather … Paige had had run-ins with the desk sergeants and dispatchers at the sheriff's department in the past. This time, instead of slamming her way in bombastically, she entered the office as quietly as a penitent.

When Paige entered, Deputy Chris Holland was sitting up front. She'd had dealings with Holland in the past, and she could see him brace himself.

Paige smiled sweetly. "I understand that my brother is here," she said calmly, looking around as though she expected him to be sitting there waiting for her.

"Uh, yes, ma'am, he's in a holding cell in back."

Paige swallowed hard, nodding her head. "A holding cell?"

"Yes, ma'am." Holland picked up a piece of paper from his desk. "He's been arrested on suspicion of murder."

"MURDER?" exclaimed Paige loudly. She felt a shifting under her coat as her loud exclamation woke Ralph.

She closed her eyes, took several deep breaths, and with an effort brought herself under control. "Murder?" she asked more calmly.

"Yes, ma'am. Detective Brooks brought him in wearing handcuffs and booked him."

"Can I see him?" asked Paige.

"Detective Brooks?" asked Holland.

"NO! My brother, you idiot!" she shouted.

A muffled voice from under Paige's coat sounded off. "Awrkk, Idiot! Idiot murder!"

When she didn't offer an explanation the deputy looked at her strangely. "Ma'am," said Holland, "in your present state of mind, I don't know if that'd be a good idea."

Paige rocked as though about to explode. Then she took several more deep breaths, forced a smile onto her face, and said, "Deputy, please, I would like to see my brother."

With a resigned countenance he said, "Well, yes, ma'am. Okay." He buzzed her in through the locked door. "Right this way, Miss Paige."

As they walked back to the cells, Holland said, "He's kind of a little the worse for wear."

Paige began a slow burn. "What do you mean? Did you guys 'tune him up'?"

"Ma'am?"

"Did he fall down a flight of stairs in this one-story building?"

"Huh? Oh! No, ma'am. Nothing like that. It's just ... well, he was pretty drunk, and he did jump in the water and try to escape, so's we had to put him in a jumpsuit. But didn't nobody lay a hand on him. 'Cept to tackle him when he tried to run after comin' outta the water. But he's okay. Just some hungover and damp."

They rounded the corner to the holding cells. There, curled up on a cot in his Northampton County Jail orange jumpsuit, looking like a giant pumpkin and snoring like a Stihl chainsaw, lay her big brother, Billy."

Deputy Holland stepped to the cell. He took a black-handled object and, with a quick flick of his wrist, opened a telescoping metal baton. He loudly banged on the bars announcing, "Wake up, Reese. You got a visitor."

Billy launched straight up as though he'd been shocked. "What the ..."

Paige looked at Holland. "You ass!"

Deputy Holland laughed and went back to the front.

Billy looked like crap, and his attitude matched. He looked at Paige through the bars.

"Well, little sister, you happy now? You see where you got me?"

"Where I got you?" she countered. "I'm not the one who started a fight with a stranger. A stranger who, I might add, is now lying on a slab in my cooler."

"And you think I killed him?"

"No, of course not, Billy."

"Then why'd you sic that detective on me?"

"I didn't 'sic' him on you. But if I hadn't told him about your fight, he would have found out when he started asking around."

"Well ..."

"And why on earth did you try to escape? Jumped in the water? Then ran?"

"I don't know, Paige. Seemed like the thing to do at the time."

"Yeah. And 'at the time' how drunk were you?"

"Well, I'd a had a few beers."

"Were you in swapping lies and beers with the Beer-Thirty Gang?"

Billy nodded his head and let it hang down.

Red-faced with fury Paige gripped the bars of the cell as though she was going to bend them open to get at Billy. "So you got shit-faced drunk and full of yourself, and when the law shows up you figured to do a Butch Cassidy and run for it? Showing off for your drinking buddies?"

"Now, Paige, that's not fair. I … I … I guess I sort of freaked out when that detective handcuffed me. I ain't never been hand-cuffed before. You know that."

Paige shook her head mournfully. "So now what?" she asked.

Billy looked at her. "Well, that's what I was going to ask you. Now what? How're you gonna get me outta here?"

"Get you out of here? Are you going back to your Butch Cassidy persona? Get you out of here? Billy, you've been charged with murder, don't you know that?"

"But, Paige, you know I didn't do it."

"Billy, I don't think they're going to put me on the jury. Have you talked to a lawyer yet?"

"A lawyer? I … I didn't think I needed a lawyer. I ain't done nothing wrong. C'mon, Paige, get me outta here."

"Oh, Billy! You really stuck your foot in it this time. You're going to have to stay here for now. I doubt they'd give you bail if you're an escape risk. I'll see what I can do. Can I bring you anything?"

He smiled wryly. "How about a cake with a hacksaw in it?"

Paige laughed. "I'll come by tomorrow with some toiletries and stuff. Maybe I'll bring you a book to read."

"Yeah! And would you go by Yuk Yuk's and get me a cheeseburger and fries?"

"Sure. And I'll talk to Tim and see if he has any suggestions."

"Yeah, great."

Billy shuffled to the bars. "Thanks, Paige," he said. "I'm sorry for all of this."

"Okay. I'll see you tomorrow."

On her way out, Paige stopped at the front. "Can I bring him some clothes so he doesn't have to wear that orange jumpsuit?"

Holland shook his head. "Ain't Club Med back there. He'll wear what we give him and do what we tell him."

"Well, damn it!" stormed Paige.

From within the confines of her jacket came an echoing, "Awwrkk, damn it! Damn it!"

"What the hell is that?" demanded Deputy Holland, and Paige quickly slipped out the door.

Fifteen

TIM GLANCED AT his phone's caller ID as he sat at his desk. He was happy to see that Paige was calling him from Eastville, across The Bay.

"Hey, there, farm girl," he said. "Time to milk the cows?"

"Tim, I'm so glad you're there," answered a harried-sounding Paige.

"Paige! What's the matter?" he asked.

"Detective Brooks has arrested my brother for murder. They've locked him in the jail. I don't know what to do."

"First off, take three slow deep breaths," said Tim.

Paige complied, her breath sounding loud over the phone line.

"Now, tell me what's going on."

She sighed. "You were with me when I found out about Billy fighting with that man, that Guy Coleman. I knew that as ineffective as Detective Brooks is, he's still smart enough to find that out, too. You were with me when I told him about it, hoping to kind of ease the information into him so he wouldn't race off with Billy in his sights."

"Yes," said Tim.

"Didn't work. You guys raced down to Mallard Cove, and Brooks arrested him. Of course, then my half-wit brother tried to escape by jumping in the water. Now he's sitting in the county jail. Tim, I just don't know what to do."

"I'll be there in an hour," responded Tim.

"But what can you do?" asked Paige.

"I'm not sure, beyond holding your hand and comforting you. I'd just feel better over there with you as we're going through this."

"Oh, Tim! You're sweet. But don't come if it is going to cause you any trouble with your Special Agent in Charge."

"I'll bring a briefcase of paperwork with me," he said. "It'll be a semi-official working trip."

"Well, okay. I've gotta admit I'd feel better with you over here."

"See you soon."

It was well after midnight when Tim arrived at Paige's apartment on Wilkins Beach. Traffic was always light at that time of the morning on The Shore, and he had, admittedly, pushed the speed limit a bit to hurry.

Paige must have been waiting for him because she flung open her apartment door before he could even knock.

She threw herself into his arms weeping. "What am I going to do?"

Ralph had been balanced on her shoulder when she threw herself at Tim and ended up catapulted onto Tim's shoulder. He promptly showed his displeasure with this behavior by latching onto Tim's earlobe.

"Ow, hey!" exclaimed Tim, and flailed at the bird on his shoulder.

Paige managed a laugh. "Ralph!" she said scoldingly. "You know Tim. Let him go right now!"

You cannot train a parrot like you can a Pekingese, but Ralph chose at that moment to let go of Tim's ear and fly back into the apartment where he perched on the shade of a couch-side lamp, muttering to himself.

"You look like you had your ear pierced," giggled Paige. "Do you want to borrow a gold stud to keep it open?"

Tim was not amused.

"That hurt," he complained. "Damn bird!"

"Awwrkk, damn it! Damn it! Damn idiot!" answered Ralph.

Paige giggled as she put some ice in a dishtowel for Tim's lacerated earlobe. Then she grew serious. "Tim, I just have no idea what to do to help Billy. What do you think?"

"I think the first thing is to get him a lawyer."

"But he's innocent," said Paige.

Tim sat in a chair far from the lamp where Ralph perched.

"There are lots of innocent men in prison, Paige," said Tim.

"Oh, thanks lots," she snapped.

"I mean, just because *we* know he didn't do anything doesn't mean a thing if this goes to a jury. Let's face it, he had motive."

Paige flopped down on the couch and buried her face in her hands. "I know. I'm sorry. It's just ... I feel like I need to do something."

"Paige, the best thing you and I can do right now is to find who really did commit the murder. That's of the utmost importance."

Hearing one of his trigger words Ralph chimed in, "Murder idiot! Awwrkk."

"But how do we do that?"

"Paige, for being an undertaker, you're one of the best sleuths I know. Especially in this special area of The Eastern Shore. We'll use your special talents and knowledge and find the guilty party. Then they'll have to let Billy go."

"And he can go back to being unreliable beer-oriented Billy, living like an alcoholic hermit on that boat of his."

"C'mon, Paige. Give him a break. You're just angry with him for getting into this mess, and it probably isn't even his fault."

"Yeah, you're right. Poor dumb slob."

"Awwrkk, dumb slob! Dumb slob!"

"You've got that right, Ralph."

She turned to Tim. "Okay, where do we start?"

PAIGE HELPED TIM clear the SOUTHERN LIVING magazines off the coffee table in front of the couch. Sitting on the end of the couch, away from Ralph, he opened his brief-case and took out a thick sheaf of papers.

"I think that the first thing we must do," he said, "is to pos-itively identify the victim and try to figure out exactly what he was doing in Cape Charles."

Paige nodded in agreement.

Tim continued, "Then, hopefully, we'll be able to determine what motive someone had for killing him."

"Okay," said Paige.

"Then we hopefully can use that knowledge to figure out just where the murder took place. If we can get the 'why and where,' we'll be that much further along to determine the 'who.'"

"Sounds like a plan to me," agreed Paige. "Where do we start?"

"Right here," said Tim as he gestured at the thick pile of documents. "These are all the documents Coleman had in his briefcase at the Hotel Cape Charles. A lot of them were in Chinese, so I got one of our people to translate them for me."

"But this isn't an FBI case, is it?" asked Paige.

"I called in a favor."

"Have you read them yet?"

"No," replied Tim. "I was just about to start in on them when I got your distress call. I threw them all in my case and raced on over."

"Sorry 'bout that," said Paige, looking guilty.

"Not at all," said Tim. "I'd rather be here with you than in my empty office. And it gives me the added bonus of someone famil-iar with the case that I can bounce ideas off of. It's a win-win."

Paige smiled. She wasn't sure whether he was just being gracious, but he did make her feel wanted and useful.

"I think that the translated Chinese papers might be most probative," opined Tim, "but let's start with the ones in English to try to establish a basis on which we can build."

Paige went to the kitchen and made them each a strong cup of coffee, which she put on the coffee table along with a plate of cookies. She figured they'd need the caffeine and sugar.

They sat side-by-side on the couch, reading the documents and passing them back and forth while sipping at their coffee. In the quiet, Ralph became restless and flew to his cage where Paige had put several toys for him. He especially loved the gym she had bought from Amazon (in a frantic next-day delivery when she realized how rambunctious he was) and enjoyed hanging upside down and swinging from the trapeze while whistling *La Cucaracha*.

Tim and Paige compared documents and ideas.

"Okay, Coleman was Vice President for Acquisition for a wind-energy company headquartered in Pensacola, Florida," observed Tim. "From the copies of articles from THE CAPE CHARLES MIRROR, it's obvious that the Commonwealth of Virginia has approved construction of a huge wind farm. But it's supposed to be twenty-seven miles offshore from Virginia Beach, and this guy's company is not the one building it."

"Okay, now what?" asked Paige.

"These cost studies show that building onshore wind farms, even with the added cost of land acquisition, is a lot more cost-effective than having to build 300-foot-tall towers in hundreds of feet of water. But the offshore wind farm is over 1000 acres, and there's not that much land available onshore."

"Okay …" said Paige, still not following.

"Let's look at these documents that were in Chinese."

Unexpectedly there was a knock at the door. "Who on earth could that be?" asked Paige as she rose to answer it. Walking to the door, she called out, "Hello?" There was no answer. Again, "hello?" Nothing. Paige looked through the peephole in the door but could not see anyone.

"There's no one there," she said to Tim.

"Hang on a minute," said Tim as he joined her at the door. After looking through the peephole and seeing nothing, Tim pushed Paige away from the door, and with his hand on his weapon, eased the door open. Nothing. Tim pulled the door fully open and stepped through, joined by Paige. There was no one there.

Then they heard the knocking again … from within the apartment!

"Ralph, was that you?" demanded Paige, back in the apartment.

Ralph just hung upside down, unconcernedly, and sang,

♩♩ "*Ay, ay, ay, ay,*
    Canta y no llores,
    Porque cantando se alegran,
    cielito lindo, los corazones."

Tim stifled a laugh. "Easy, Paige. You look ready to pluck Ralph down to a bare nubbin." He laughed, and although she tried not to, she joined him in the guffawing.

"Damn bird," she said.

"Awwrkk, damn it! Damn it!"

They returned to reading the translated documents. Ralph returned to whistling *La Cucaracha*.

"Paige," said Tim, somewhat tentatively, "from these Chinese documents, it appears that our victim was over here trying to acquire land for an onshore wind farm."

Paige nodded in agreement.

"But the only land he was looking at was land in the Eastern Shore National Wildlife Refuge and on the Barrier Islands."

"But that's not available," said Paige. "The National Wildlife Refuge is owned by the federal government, and the Barrier Islands all belong to the Nature Conservancy. They bought them up to keep something like this from happening."

This time Tim nodded. "But it looks like that's what they're trying to do. Look at this: it's how much money Coleman had available to offer for the rights to build in those areas."

"Bribe money!" exclaimed Paige.

"Well, we can't say that for sure. Yet. But it certainly looks unsavory."

"What can we do now?"

"Right now we can get some sleep. It is rather late. Then in the morning, we can keep digging through this briefcase," said Tim.

"The guest room is all yours," said Paige. "And I'll throw a cover over Ralph's cage. That'll help keep him quiet until we get up."

"Sounds good to me," said Tim. He kissed Paige on the cheek. He waved at Ralph, "Good night, roomie," he called.

"Awwrkk! Damn bird!"

Sixteen

IT WAS EARLY morning, before dawn, and Nott was beach-combing. Of course, it now being late October, dawn was coming later and later. And the breeze off the water was right chilly. But he had on his white rubber boots, a ratty old Army field jacket, and a nasty stained Sewansecott Oyster Company ball cap, so he was toasty warm. All but his face, that is.

Today his "shopping" had taken him south past Custis Tomb to the beach at Pickett's Harbor. Since the Coast Guard had approved the deep-water anchorage off Cape Charles and allowed it to fill with foreign-flagged vessels, Nott never knew what sort of jetsam would float up on the shore. He was used to crab floats and the like, but now he often would find good wood planks pried from packing crates stenciled with foreign words. There was exotic trash, and one time even an unopened bottle of Japanese beer. Sapporo, he thought he remembered.

He walked south on the beach, hands deep in his pockets, not thinking about much beyond what he might find. So far, pickings had been very lean. Well, it could be that way at times. And other times he'd be lucky and manage to scrounge up something valuable to his lifestyle. That's how he'd gotten his boat, an abandoned hulk washed up near Cape Charles. And once when he found a wrecked cruising sailboat, about a thirty-five-footer, Nott managed to salvage the alcohol stove. He now cooked over that stove, and he'd also found the candle lantern he used to light his home. He'd had his periods of luck, so he couldn't complain when the winds and the waves left him empty-handed once in a while.

Down the beach, toward the Kiptopeke State Park land, something fluttered bright orange in the sand. It was too small to be a lost life jacket, but it was the right color. He walked on, unhurried.

When he arrived at the spot, he saw that the fluttering orange was a long strip of surveyor's tape attached to a three-foot-long two-inch by two-inch pine stake. Several of the tasseled stakes lay on the sand. At least two dozen. They looked like the kind of stakes a surveyor would use to plot out a new development, and he could see by their discolored spiked bottoms that they had been driven into the sand somewhere. But Nott was familiar with what was happening on The Shore. It was very much a small-town community, and he wasn't aware of any developments planned or abandoned.

Well, the stakes might come in handy for something, and it was a shame just to leave them here to rot or wash away. At the very least, Nott could give them to Betty Mapp or another of the young people to have a bonfire on the beach up to Cape Charles. So, he bundled the stakes into his arms and carried them back to his boat.

Seventeen

PAIGE AWOKE TO the beguiling aromas of bacon and coffee. It took her a minute to remember why. Then she heard a quiet voice talking softly to Ralph, and she remembered. Tim had spent the night in her guest room.

Making enough noise that he would know she was up, she went into her *en suite* bathroom and showered. Yesterday had been a tortuously long day, and when she finally got to bed in the wee hours of the morning, she was just too exhausted to shower. Now a good hot shower would be rejuvenating and get her properly set up for a new day. She was feeling great … until she remembered brother Billy. While she was standing in a hot shower, he'd be sitting all alone in a Northampton County jail cell. Like as not feeling put upon, deserted, and miserably sorry for himself.

Well, she thought, *that certainly took the pleasure out of my shower.* She reached out, and as a penance turned the hot water off. She'd suffer like her poor brother was suffering.

As the first drops of icy water hit her shoulders she decided that Billy could suffer by himself and quickly jumped out of the now frigid water. Whew! What had she been thinking? This was no romance novel that required her to make such a sacrifice!

She toweled off vigorously to get her circulation flowing. Pulling on blue jeans and a William and Mary hooded sweatshirt, she went out to the kitchen.

"Hey, sleepyhead," greeted Tim.

Upon seeing her, Ralph let out a pleased chirp, flew to her shoulder, then climbed down into her sweatshirt hood to curl up in its warmth.

"He knows where to go," chuckled Tim.

"Yeah," said Paige. "So, what's up?"

"Breakfast. I hope you like bacon and eggs. I thought about going up to Kate's Kupboard, but I was afraid birdbrain, there, would wake you when I left. So I turned domestic."

"As much as I *adore* Kate's sticky buns, they do a real job on my hips," said Paige. Then she blushed. TMI — too much information. Tim wasn't a stranger, but they certainly were not at the secret intimacies stage.

But Tim didn't seem to notice. "I love them too, but I thought with all of the work we have ahead of us today, we should probably have something more substantial. Although that sugar rush does help get the brain firing."

Paige laughed. "Just put an extra teaspoon of sugar in your coffee."

"Actually, I found this jar of honey in your cabinet. It's got even more of a kick."

"Mmmm. Me too, please."

They pointedly avoided discussing the case as they ate break-fast. Get the day off positively, she thought. But the problem was still hanging around them like a black cloud, and as soon as they had done the breakfast dishes (Tim insisted that since he had dirtied them, he should wash them), they moved to the living room couch and the papers on the coffee table.

"I haven't had a chance to look at these documents that are translated from Chinese," said Tim. "Hopefully we can find something there that will shed a little light on who our Mr. Coleman is and what he did to get himself killed."

"Let's start digging," replied Paige.

They spent the next two hours reading documents, handing them back and forth between one another, pointing out indi-vidual paragraphs or sentences, and drinking copious amounts of coffee. They didn't talk much, mostly making grunts and "hmmms" as they read.

Finally, Paige said, "I can't do this anymore. You wanna go out for lunch, or do you want me to fix something here?"

"I saw your larder," said Tim. "Unless I want a mayo-and-mustard sandwich on white with catsup, I think we'd better go out."

"Great!" said Paige. "I'm in the mood for a softshell crab sandwich up to the Exmore Diner. That suit you?"

"Well, it's a bit of a drive, but sure. We've been working hard. We deserve the break. It'll help get the cobwebs out of our heads."

They spent two hours over their lunch, including time to drop a cheeseburger and French fries off for Billy at the jail.

They didn't go back to see how he was doing. He'd been so pathetic and pitiful the day before that Paige just didn't want to see him. That and Ralph was still snuggled in her sweatshirt hood, and she didn't want a repeat of his almost getting caught by the deputy.

Back at her apartment, Paige reached into her hood and pulled Ralph out. He yawned at her, and she took him over to his cage. "Get in there," she said, and he walked into the cage and up onto his play gym. She didn't bother to close the cage door. Ralph had figured out how to open the cage door the first night, and now the only way to ensure he stayed in there was to drape the cover over the cage. The darkness was a soporific for the little bird.

Back on the couch, Paige turned to Tim and asked, "So? Whaddya think?"

Tim shook his head. "Paige," he began, "I don't want to jump to any rash assumptions here ..."

"Jump!" urged Paige.

Tim smiled.

"It appears that Mr. Coleman's company, I-HAWK, which is owned by the Chinese, was not satisfied with the auction of the offshore plot for the wind farm and has decided to try to build a competing wind farm but do it onshore. And our late Mr. Coleman was here to scout out locations and attempt acquisition of the required land."

"Okay," said Paige. "I can follow that. But we're talking about what, 1000 acres? There's not that much property available down here."

"Not in private hands, maybe. But there're over 1100 acres in the National Wildlife Reserve, and I don't know how many acres on the Barrier Islands. Not to mention the shallow waters between the Islands and the mainland."

"Of course, but that's all protected. No one is allowed to do any development in there."

Tim replied, "But there are those who say that a wind farm is the 'highest and best use' for the property. And they say that the footprint of a wind farm isn't destructive. They point to the west where they still run cattle actually under the towers of wind farms."

"Well, this isn't Wyoming," responded Paige. "And how about the flyway?"

"A wind farm is kind of rough on the birds. This big of a farm in the middle of the Atlantic Flyway might kill a half-million birds in a year. But people say, 'that's only dumb birds.'"

"Awwrkk, dumb bird, dumb bird."

They ignored him.

"But that's why all this land is protected. They can't buy it, right?"

"No, but money talks. And apparently, the Chinese have put enough money into this enterprise that they think they can influence things. How many politicians do you think they'd have to buy to get permission?"

Paige felt aghast. "But ... but the lands are protected!"

"Until they aren't," responded Tim cynically. "A little gift here, and emolument there, and 'Presto!' Things change."

"We've got to stop them, Tim. We can't let them do it. We've got to notify the Citizens for a Better Eastern Shore. We've got to call Donna and get her people mobilized." She jumped to her feet and headed for the telephone.

"Wait a minute, Paige. I thought our primary focus was getting Billy out of jail."

She stopped short. "Oh, yeah."

"And to do that we have to find out who killed Guy Coleman."

Paige let out a deep sigh. "Oh, yeah, that too."

"And to help with that we've got to find out where he was killed and who would be the one most likely to benefit from his demise."

"Oh, Tim," she wailed. "We've got so much to do. How are we going to get it all done?" And sobbing, she buried her head in his shoulder.

Eighteen

IT WAS MID-AFTERNOON, and Tim and Paige felt mentally fried. They had been reading the documents from Coleman's attaché case for hours and were getting no closer to figuring out the murder. Why was he killed? Where was he killed? For that matter, how had he been killed?

"Tell you what," said Tim. "Let's borrow Jim Baugh's flats boat and run out to Nott's. We can take him to dinner and talk all of this over with him. It's always nice to have another brain percolating on these things."

"And we can have him pack his things and stay at my apartment up in town," said Paige. "I doubt that he's got anything else on his schedule. And we did say that we needed to take him out for a meal, get him out of his hermitage."

"Sounds good to me."

An hour later they were idling up to Nott's oyster guardhouse in the middle of Cherrystone Creek. Since Nott never turned on his iPhone, they couldn't check with him. They were relieved to see his scow tied to one of the legs supporting the house.

Nott heard them coming up the creek and was waiting for them at the top of the stairs up from the water.

"Hey, y'all. What's happenin'?" he called to them as they cut the engine on their boat and drifted up to the piling.

"Pack your duffel bag, Nott. We'd like you to come ashore and help us with this investigation for a couple of days. You can stay up town at Paige's."

"You didn't have anything else planned, did you?" called Paige.

Nott shook his head and laughed. "Lemme check my appointments secretary." He paused for effect. "No, I guess I'm free for a while."

Paige and Tim both smiled. It hadn't been too long ago that Nott was an almost total recluse. Paige had more-or-less adopted him, like one would a beaten dog at the pound, and brought him out of his shell. He still had occasional flashbacks, but they were getting much less often and significantly milder.

Nott considered the apartment upstairs over Paige's funeral home, his "onshore" home.

Tim climbed up to Nott's stilt-house to help him with his kit and noticed the large pile of engineer stakes on the leeward side of the house.

"What are these, Nott?" he asked.

"I found them all on the beach down to Pickett's Harbor," answered Nott. "Don't know where they came from or what I'm gonna do with them but seemed wasteful just to leave them there to rot."

"Engineer stakes, aren't they?" asked Tim.

"Look to be," Nott responded. Coming out of the house toting his well-worn Army-green duffel bag, he said, "Okay. I'm ready."

"You're not going to lock your door?" asked Tim.

Nott laughed at him. "Them stakes are prob'ly the most valuable thing out here, 'ceptin' my boat. And anybody poor enough to steal that … well, they're welcome to it." He climbed down into his scow.

"Hey," said Paige, leaning forward to give him a peck on the cheek. "Don't you want to ride with us?"

"Naw," said Nott. "I like to keep my options open. I'll tie up over to the city dock."

Before they left, Paige leaned over and called to Nott, "Where do you want to eat?"

"Anything but fish or crab," he answered. "Out here, that and Dinty Moore Beef Stew are about all I eat. I think I'd like a burger and a beer."

"Done," said Paige. "We'll go to Cape Charles Brewery."

While Tim and Paige both enjoyed crab cake sandwiches, Nott was in epicurean heaven with a Black and Bleu Burger, the juices running down his chin.

"You know, you're the one that started this whole mess," said Paige looking at Nott.

Poor Nott, still a bit tender when it came to poking fun, almost choked on a bite of his burger. "What? What thing?"

Paige dipped a fry in her ketchup then swirled it through a puddle of mayonnaise. "Tim's helping me with the investigation of that body you found buried on the beach."

"Hey, I didn't find him. That was the dozer driver. I just happened to be the one to notify Sergeant Heath. Almost didn't, you know. After they tried to pin that little girl's death on me, I almost just let this one go."

"But you couldn't," said Paige. "That's because you're a good person."

Nott blushed slightly.

"Well, how can I help this time?" he asked.

"Let's wait until we get up to Paige's," replied Tim. "Then we can show you what all we've done so far."

When they walked into Paige's beachfront apartment, Tim and Nott headed for the couch, and Paige walked over to the covered cage in the corner. It was getting easier to convince Ralph to stay behind if she gave him one of his favorite treats — a piece of buffalo jerky — then put him in his covered cage. She took the cover from the cage and opened the unlocked door, turning to walk to the couch. Ralph exited his jail and flew to her shoulder. He snuggled up to her ear and let loose with a manufactured but very realistic b-u-r-r-r-p.

"Good gracious, Ralph. Show some manners," scolded Paige.

Just then Pongo, the 18-pound Maine Coon Cat, came slinking around the corner, curious to see who all was in *his* living room. Ralph hopped down onto the coffee table and glared at him.

"Watch this," said Paige quietly.

Pongo issued a deep quiet growl as he crouched down, staring hard at the seemingly nonchalant Ralph. Just the tip of Pongo's tail moved, but it twitched furiously.

Pongo started inching toward Ralph when suddenly Ralph fluffed out all his feathers, making his body seem twice as big. He spread his wings, glared at Pongo, and screeched like fingernails on a blackboard. The three on the couch were so surprised by the volume of Ralph's shriek they all jumped. Pongo ... well, poor Pongo went about three feet straight up in the air. At the height of his leap, he performed a feline Immelmann and raced for his sanctuary under the guest room bed.

All Tim could say was, "Wow!"

Nott just sat there, stunned.

Paige chuckled. "Okay, entertainment's over. Let's try to get some work done before it gets too late."

Bringing Nott up to speed on where they were proved a valuable tool, as it enabled them to review and reinforce everything they'd found so far.

"Let me summarize," said Nott. "First, we have a body buried on the beach. An unknown man whose jewelry and wallet have been removed to make identification more difficult and to make it look like a robbery."

The other two nodded.

Nott continued, "The body was wrapped in Visqueen or some similar heavy construction plastic sheet."

"Right," said Paige.

"And there were holes in the Visqueen where it had been torn off some type of construction it was protecting."

Paige looked at Tim. "Didn't think of that," she said.

"So, where did the Visqueen come from?" asked Nott. "I think that should be one of our first questions. Might help us figure out where he was killed."

"Damn," said Paige.

"Awwrkk! Damn it! Damn it!"

"Not now, Ralph!" She turned to Nott. "Where's there construction going on? Nott, do you know of any buildings be built or undergoing major work?"

"No, Paige. 'Course with no car I don't get around much to see, ya know?"

Paige slowly nodded. "Well, I don't think they're doing anything at Bay Creek since real estate sales have flattened."

She thought for a moment. "I guess there could always be something going up over on Seaside Road. I don't get over there too much. Of course, I always think 'south.' Maybe it's north. Something in Machipongo or Nassawadox. But I don't know of anything major."

Nott rubbed his stubbled chin. "Maybe we should check with the hardware stores and see if anyone bought it out here on The Shore."

"Whew!" said Tim. "That'd be a chore. And there are all the outlets just across The Bay in Norfolk and Little Creek, too. Might have to do that, but let's try something else first."

Paige snapped her fingers. "I know! Let's talk to Gordon Campbell. He helped out so much in the aerial search for —"

She gulped, "—for me. Maybe he's seen something while he's been flying over the area. Or, worse comes to worst, maybe we can charter him to search the area for new construction."

"Great idea, Paige," said Tim smiling at her. "If we have to get him to search do you want to fly shotgun this time?"

"You bet I do. Donna had all the fun last time."

By now it was getting late again, and everyone was beginning to yawn. The yawning was infectious and even Ralph was yawning — loudly.

"I'll drive Nott up town to his apartment," said Paige, "and get him the keys to the truck. You sleeping in the guest room with Pongo, Tim?"

"Yeah. At least Pongo doesn't attack me like your dumb bird."

"Awwrkk, dumb bird! Dumb bird!"

Nott laughed, not having seen this performance before.

Tim eyed the bird. "I'm not sure I feel comfortable being alone with him.

Ralph started whistling *La Cucaracha* again.

Nineteen

EARLY THE NEXT morning Nott knocked on the door to Paige's apartment at Wilkins Beach. Tim opened the door and waved him in. Paige was in the kitchen cooking breakfast, Ralph perched on her shoulder, head turned back to keep a beady eye on Nott.

As they sat down to bacon, eggs, and cheese grits, Tim said, "Thanks to Nott's precision, we now know where square one is for us. We have to figure out where the Visqueen came from. That should, and I repeat *should* give us an idea of where the murder might have happened. We need that to start unraveling this rat's nest."

Paige swallowed a mouthful of grits and agreed. "Yeah, Tim, when you and I were presented with a murdered body, we immediately went off in the wrong direction."

"We thought that the first thing to solving this mess was to identify the victim. And that was important," said Tim, "but equally important was to determine where the crime had occurred. Those two together would give us a much better base on which to build our conjectures."

"Whew!" said Nott. "'Base on which to build our conjectures.' You sound like an FBI agent."

"Sorry," smiled Tim. "Sometimes I get carried away."

Paige chuckled, "Well, we've got half of step one done. How do we find where it happened?"

"I like the idea of an aerial search," said Nott. "Either Gordon Campbell, or maybe get one of the local crop dusters."

"I like the idea of Gordon and his Dragonfly. Its 46 knots should be enough to get the job done, but slow enough to see what we need," said Tim. "You'll have to bundle up, though, Paige. It's going to be cold flying up in that thing. You know you'll be sitting out in the air … no fuselage."

"I know. I'm ready. Let's call Gordon and set it up."

They met Gordon at his small airfield in Weirwood. He'd been there for a while, pre-flighting his Dragonfly and letting his Rotax 912S engine warm up. They'd previously briefed him on what they needed to do in their search, so he was ready to go.

"You going to be my spotter, Paige?" he asked.

Paige nodded, and Gordon helped her aboard, fastening her into the seat. "Don't want you to go flying without me should we hit a speed bump up there," he said, smiling.

Gordon revved the engine and they bumped down the winter-browned stubble of the grass field and into the air.

Gordon leaned over and shouted to Paige, "Since we're already up here, I thought we could start north and work our way down to the Bridge-Tunnel."

She gave him a thumbs up.

"We'll have to come back for re-fueling, though." The Dragonfly only carried six gallons of fuel and would suck that down pretty quickly, going full speed with two people on board.

"You're covered," yelled back Paige. She looked like she was dressed for an Arctic expedition. She had on a well-padded ski suit, a knit watch cap with a long tassel, heavy gloves, goggles, and Pac Boots on her feet.

Flying east over Woodstock to the coast, they turned north. When they got to Willis Wharf, Gordon took a smooth left turn to head west across the peninsula. Once they flew over Exmore and the highway they were back into farmland and the occasional vineyard.

"What's that?" asked Paige, pointing.

They turned slightly. "That's David's Nursery," said Gordon. "They use lots of plastic in some of their fields to keep weeds from growing, but it's definitely not as heavy as Visqueen."

Paige nodded her understanding, and they turned a touch more southerly, flying over more fields and forests until they got to the water. Then they flew south until they were just above Silver Beach when they turned back east for the next leg of their search.

They kept up this ladder-like search pattern until Gordon tapped the fuel gauge for Paige to look. He turned them north and landed back at his field in Weirwood to refuel.

Tim and Nott were waiting for them. "Find anything?" asked Tim.

"No, not yet."

"I talked to my buddy down to Scott Farm," said Gordon. "He's going to let us refuel there where he keeps his duster. That'll save us time, not having to come all the way back up here."

"Great," said Paige. "We ready?"

"You staying warm enough?" asked Tim.

"I'm fine," she said. "Let's go."

Back in the air Paige leaned over to Gordon. "I want to take a good look at Bay Creek. If anyone is doing construction, it should be right there." Gordon nodded his assent.

But there wasn't anything to see there. Legal wrangles and depressed real estate sales had long ago quieted the work at Bay Creek.

They continued their search, refueling again at Scott's.

Paige was getting discouraged. And cold. Fields and forests and cold air.

"Getting ready to call it quits?" asked Gordon.

"No, we've spent hours at this. Let's finish down to the Bridge-Tunnel then fly over Smith, Cobb, and Hog Islands on the way home."

"Nothing to see out on the barrier islands, Paige."

"Yeah, I know. But let's do it. I love the islands. I just want to see them from your Dragonfly, Gordon."

"Okay. It's your dollar and your pneumonia."

They kept up their crisscross search pattern until they got over the Eastern Shore National Wildlife Refuge.

"Got to be real careful down here," said Gordon. "This is prime migration time. Don't want to tangle any birds in my propeller."

Paige nodded her agreement. She was enjoying this part of the flight, though. There were lots of birds to see, and many of them were flying at their altitude. It gave her the feeling of being a hawk, hovering over the deserted scrubland below. Then, "What's that?" exclaimed Paige pointing to a wooden structure in the Refuge.

Gordon banked around and decreased their speed and altitude.

"It's a new wooden bird-watching blind," said Paige. "And the roof is covered with Visqueen! See that?"

Gordon nodded. "Seen enough for now?"

Paige was ecstatic. Maybe this was it. "Yeah, let's head back. But I'd still like to swing out over the islands. Okay?"

"Sure," called back Gordon as he headed northeast toward the Atlantic and the barrier islands.

They crossed over Magothy and Smith Island Bays and the tidal flats and soon were watching the Atlantic surf frothing whitely as it crashed onto Smith Island. Cold as the air was it was tangy with salt and smelled fresh and enjoyable. Paige loved it.

Then she saw it. "Gordon, circle back for a moment."

"Paige, we don't have a lot of fuel to play around."

"Go back, Gordon. I saw something."

Again, Gordon banked around. "Where?"

Pointing, Paige said, "Right there. You see them?"

Gordon did. There in the deserted isolation of Smith Island was a line of what looked like engineer's stakes with long orange streamers blowing from them.

"What the heck, Gordon? The Nature Conservancy owns these islands. Nobody can develop them, can they?"

Gordon just shook his head and turned them toward his field, 22 miles distant. As they flew north, they could see lines of engineer stakes on Wreck and Cobb Islands, also.

Paige was perplexed. The Nature Conservancy had bought almost all the Virginia Barrier Islands to preserve them from developers turning them into something hideous like the Jersey Shore. Now there were all these stakes there. What was happening?

Back on the ground in Weirwood, Paige thanked Gordon then hustled Tim and Nott into their car. She couldn't hide her upset feelings from the guys.

"What happened, Paige?" asked Tim, looking concerned. "Did you come up empty? No Visqueen?"

"OH!" said Paige. "I almost forgot. Yeah, I found Visqueen. They are using it on the new bird-watching blinds down in the Refuge."

"Wow," said Nott. "Great. Somewhere to get started."

"There's something else, though," said Paige. "I had Gordon fly back by way of the barrier islands."

"Yeah?" said Nott.

"Out on the islands, I saw a bunch of engineer's stakes with orange streamers. THAT'S SUPPOSED TO BE PROTECTED PROPERTY! No one is allowed to develop or build out there. What's that all about?"

"Wood stakes with orange tape streamers?" asked Tim.

Paige nodded.

"Like the ones Nott found on the beach at Pickett's Harbor?"

Paige started and looked at Tim. "My gosh, just like them."

Nott glanced back and forth between them. "The mystery thickens," he said theatrically.

Twenty

BACK AT PAIGE'S apartment, they returned their attention to the thick ream of documents from Coleman's attaché case.

"So, he was working for a Chinese wind energy company?" asked Nott. "I don't know much about wind energy. It's just some big windmills, isn't it? I thought it was supposed to be safe and clean."

Paige looked at Tim. She wasn't sure, either.

"I know a little about it," said Tim. "The windmills aren't just big, Nott. They're huge. Over 300 feet tall. And the blades on the windmill are about 120 feet long each."

"Wow. That's big," said Nott.

"I don't know if you've seen the windmills on television, but the blades look like they are just lazily rotating. Truth is, they'll start generating electricity when the wind is about six miles per hour."

"How fast is our wind?" asked Nott.

"I'm not sure," said Tim. "Let's find out."

He turned to his laptop. "According to the computer, the wind speed at Cape Charles averages between six and twelve miles per hour. That's enough for a wind farm."

Paige spoke up. "What do you mean 'wind farm?'"

"From what I've read," said Tim, "it's most efficient to have a whole bunch of windmills working together. Wait, I think I saw something in here …"

He rummaged through the documents. "Here we go. From the CAPE CHARLES MIRROR,

> *The bill clears the way for the development of up to 5,200 megawatts of offshore wind, which is costlier than other forms of renewable energy, by declaring it in the public interest. Dominion currently has a small pilot project underway and has previously announced plans for a 220-turbine project in federal waters.*

"That's the wind farm they're talking about putting 27 miles off of Virginia Beach."

"220 windmills!" said Nott. "In how much space?"

"I think I read that it's about 1000 acres. So that's, I guess two towers per acre."

"1000 acres. That's the size of the National Wildlife Refuge," said Paige. "But … isn't wind power supposed to be good for the environment? Clean and green?"

"It seems that there are always unintended consequences," said Tim.

"What does that mean?" asked Nott.

Tim went on. "That's where a possibly good action brings in a bad result. For instance, someone taught Ralph how to talk. Now we can't get him to shut up. And often the words taught him as a joke are inappropriate."

"Inappropriate?" asked Nott.

Paige spoke up, "Yeah, like when he yells 'damn it' at the top of his voice when we're eating in a nice restaurant."

"Awwrkk, damn it! Damn it!"

"Yeah," said Nott.

"In the case of wind energy," said Tim, "production of wind energy means you need special big batteries. Making the batteries calls for all sorts of special materials, like lithium. Obtaining those materials, usually in South America or other third world countries, often means using methods that are destructive to the environment."

"Oh, I get it," said Nott.

"In that case, the actual production of the electricity isn't bad, but the *unintended consequences* are quite destructive."

"What else?" asked Paige.

"Well, there's a study going on up in New England to see if wind farms in the ocean have any effect on the commercial fishing industry. And land-based wind farms ... well, they kill birds."

"What?" exclaimed Paige.

"That's one reason it would be so bad to have a wind farm in the Wildlife Refuge. It wouldn't have a lot of negative effects on the earth itself, but those turbines kill birds. One estimate I read in these papers was that wind turbines kill over 500,000 birds a year. We're right in the Atlantic Flyway. If they put up a wind farm here the results could be catastrophic in the number of bird deaths. And not just gulls. Hawks, bald eagles, ducks, pelicans — everything that passes through here on their annual migrations."

"That's why these areas are supposed to be protected," said Paige. "Do you honestly think Coleman was here trying to scout for locations for a wind farm? How would he get the permits?"

"I think that's where the China connection comes in. The Chinese own Coleman's company and they have deep pockets. If we can prove that they are funding this, bankrolling bribes to officials to get permits, then it becomes a Federal case."

"Oh, all right!" enthused Paige.

"But first, let's go down to the Wildlife Refuge and sniff around ... see if we can determine if that actually is where the murder took place."

THEY DIDN'T TALK much on the drive down to the Eastern Shore of Virginia National Wildlife Refuge. Each lost in his own thoughts about what was happening—each wondering who would have to get paid off for something like this to happen.

Arriving at the National Wildlife Refuge, they drove to the bird watching blind where Paige had seen the plastic sheet in use.

"There it is," said Nott.

"You think that's the same stuff, Paige?" asked Tim.

"Yeah, I'm pretty sure. And look — you can see extra corners of plastic where the first covering was torn off then replaced."

"Let's spread out and look around, then," said Tim. "See if we can find anything that might be evidence."

"What're we lookin' for?" asked Nott.

"I don't know," answered Tim. "Just ... something. Use your imagination. Anything at all that's out of place — doesn't belong here."

"Okay," said Nott, sounding doubtful.

They walked individually in ever-widening concentric circles based at the bird blind. "Is this what you meant by something out of place?" called Nott.

They quickly gathered at his side and looked down. Nott had found a deep hole. It was roughly two inches square, and you couldn't see the bottom. The critical thing was its shape. Nature doesn't like straight lines or ninety-degree angles, and this little hole was square.

"Does that look to you like a hole an engineer's stake might have made?" asked Tim.

Nott and Paige both nodded their heads.

Just then, a rustling in the brush between them and the parking area caught their attention. They smelled the smoke of strong tobacco and out stepped old Miss Mary puffing on her noxious corn cob pipe.

She squinted at them. "What yadoin' in ma Refuge?" she demanded. "Ya lookin' at ma burds?"

She turned to Tim who, remembering their last meeting, whipped off his hat and answered, "No ma'am, Miss Mary. With all respect, we are just wandering around *your* Refuge ... looking."

"Lookin' fer what, boy?"

Paige quickly inserted herself between the two potential combatants. "Miss Mary," she gushed. "It is so wonderful to see you again. Are you keepin' well?"

Old Miss Mary cocked her head and squinted one eye at Paige. "At you, Miss Paige? Shoot," she laughed, "Keepin' well? At my age? At my age ever'thin' either broke or wearin' out. You bring me any presents?"

"Oh, I'm so sorry. If I'd known we were going to see you I would have brought you something. How about the next time? What would you like?"

Old Miss Mary got a sly look on her face. "You know Coastal Baking up ta Cape Charles? They makes a praline rum mini Bundt cake ..." She grinned lasciviously. "Ya could always bring me one o' them."

"You've got it." Paige grinned back at her. "Nott, you help me remember."

"You do it, boy!" said Miss Mary. She looked back at Paige. "I can even eats it wi'out my eatin' teef in."

Paige laughed along with her.

"Miss Mary," said Paige, "have you seen any ... well, strange people out here in *your* Refuge? People who don't belong?"

"Don't nobody b'long here but me," was the reply. "Me 'n ma boy, Edd."

Paige took out a picture of Guy Coleman. "How about this man? Have you seen him here in your Refuge?"

Old Miss Mary took the picture from Paige then quickly handed it back as though it was burning her fingers. "He daid? Why you bring me the pi'cha some daid man?"

Crossing herself and muttering incantations Old Miss Mary backed away from them and disappeared into the brush.

"Well, that was less than satisfactory," said Tim.

"It's my fault," said Paige. "Old as she is, I should have realized she'd have superstitions about dead bodies. Sorry guys."

"She keeps mentioning her great-grandson, Edd," said Tim. "Does he live with her?"

"No. He's got a little house just off the Refuge. He keeps an eye on his great-grandma and tries to keep her shack livable. He's a general handyman."

"Can we go see him?" asked Tim.

"Sure," said Paige. "Let's go."

They found Edd behind his house, mending his chicken run. Edd was tall and painfully thin, dressed in overalls and a filthy canvas jacket. He wore holey sneakers on his feet, and his thin hay-colored hair stuck out in clumps from beneath a straw farm hat that had seen better days.

"Hey, Edd," called Paige.

"Paige Reese!" he responded and put down his tools. "How can I help you out?"

"We were just down to the Refuge," said Paige after introducing Tim and Nott. "Miss Mary came by, and I'm afraid we gave her a bad turn."

"Oh?"

"We were asking her if she had seen anyone strange in the Refuge. I showed her this picture and asked about him specifically."

Edd took the picture. He took off his hat and wiped a dirty hand over an equally-dirty forehead. "This guy dead?"

Paige nodded. "He's the guy they found buried on the beach in Cape Charles. We were just wondering if your grandma had seen him down there."

"Why would he have been down to the Refuge?" asked Edd.

Tim took up the story. "It looks like he works for a company that builds wind farms. He's in charge of buying up the land they need. Or maybe leasing it. We think he might have been down on the Refuge taking wind measurements and looking for sites to put up windmills."

"They cain't do that!" exclaimed Edd. "That's why it's a national refuge ... to protect it from that sort of thing."

"Yeah, but if they can convince the right people that they aren't going to hurt the land they can sometimes get permits to go ahead. Like they've got some working oil wells back in the Everglades down in Florida."

Edd shook his head sadly. "Well, I was down there workin' on thet new bird watchin' blind and I saw a bunch of guys in ties and jackets walkin' 'round."

"Really?" said Tim, excited. "Was this guy with them?" he asked motioning at the picture of Guy Coleman.

"Sorry," said Edd. "They weren't close enough for me to see." He waved at his eyes. "Gettin' old. Don't see like I useta."

"But they definitely weren't bird watchers?" asked Paige.

Edd shook his head. "No. Not dressed like they was."

"Did you maybe see them putting out engineering stakes?" asked Tim.

"You know," said Nott. "Pine stakes with orange tape on the tops?"

"No, didn't see nothing like that," replied Edd. "Listen, if'n it's okay with y'all I really gots to get back to work on this chicken coop. Varmints tryin' to get in at night and hawks during the day." He turned and started walking away.

"Okay, well thanks, Edd," called Paige.

Without looking back he just waved a hand.

"Another dead end?" asked Paige.

"We'll talk in the car," said Tim.

Twenty-one

BACK IN THE car they headed for a late lunch at Cape Charles Brewing's grill. "What are you thinking?" asked Paige.

Tim hesitated a moment. "Edd said he saw men dressed like businessmen, right?"

Paige nodded.

"Or politicians."

Nott started. "I hadn't thought about that."

"Or bureaucrats."

"Omigosh," said Paige. "Do you think those were the ones Coleman was setting up to bribe?"

"I wish we had some handle on who they were. Local or state or even federal officials?" said Tim.

He went on, "Okay, after we eat let's go visit Billy and see that he's alright. Then we'll get a mess of luminol from the sheriff's crime scene unit. After it's dark we'll go out to Nott's shack and see if there's blood on any of those stakes he found."

"How ya goin' to do that?" Nott asked.

"When you spray luminol on a surface it reacts with any blood it touches and glows blue. Like the phosphorescence you see behind your outboard motor at night on The Bay. Even if we don't see any blood on the surface, if it's there, the luminol with light it up."

"Awesome," said Nott.

"Do you think the sheriff's department will give it to us?" asked Paige.

"Well," said Tim, "I could get it from the F.B.I., but I don't want to take that long. If the sheriff resists, I'll strong-arm them."

"Let's go," said Paige.

AT THE JAIL'S front desk, Paige asked to see Billy.

"Sorry. He ain't allowed visitors," the deputy replied without even looking up.

"I'm his sister!"

"Sorry. No exceptions."

"Why not?" she demanded. "Has something happened to Billy? Did one of you 'tune him up?'"

That snapped the deputy's head up. "Ma'am, we don't do that. Best of my knowledge, he's just fine. Just not allowed any visitors."

Paige was starting to fume. "Listen, you scrawny ..."

Tim pulled her aside.

"No visitors?" he asked.

"At's right," said the deputy looking up at Tim with a jaundiced eye. "'Specially not no strangers."

It was just the opening Tim had been waiting for. Taking out his leather ID case he badged the deputy. "I am Special Agent Timothy Hannegan of the Federal Bureau of Investigation. You *will* personally escort me to Billy Reese, Junior, *right this minute*. Do you understand?"

Paige just loved it when Tim put on his FBI persona.

"Uh, ye ... yes sir!" stuttered the deputy. "Right away, sir."

Paige stayed with Tim as the deputy led them back to the holding cells. Nott had seen enough of the holding cells when he had been mistakenly locked up a while back, so he sat out front in the waiting area.

As they came around the corner to the holding cells, Paige rushed forward. "Billy!" she cried. "Billy, are you all right?"

Billy had been lying on his bunk with his back to them. He rolled over. "Paige-y!" What're you doin' here?"

"Billy, are you all right? Have they hurt you or anything?"

"Hurt me?" he asked, confused. "Heck, ain't nobody even been in to question me or nothing. I'm so bored; alls I kin do is sleep and eat. Speaking of which, did ya bring me anything to eat?"

"Oh, Billy, I'm so sorry. I didn't think of it. I'll bring something next time I come in. Cheeseburger and fries?"

"Yeah, that sounds good. But don't wait too long to come back."

"Why? Are they going to let you out?"

"No, I just don't want to have to wait too long for the cheeseburger."

Tim asked, "Billy, have you heard any jailhouse gossip about who might have murdered Coleman?"

Billy hung his head. "No," he said dejectedly. "Ever'body just assumes I done it." He looked at Paige. "But I didn't, Paige. I swear I didn't. I done a lot of dumb things in my life, but I swear I ain't never killed no one."

"I know, Billy," soothed Paige. "We're working on finding out who did. We figure that's the quickest way to get you out of here."

"Well, hurry it up. I'm dyin' here."

"Hang on. We're working on it."

Tim said, "Billy, we've got to go now. We have some actual leads we're following up on."

"Well, get at it," urged Billy.

Back out front, Tim asked to talk with the head of the crime scene unit.

"Ain't here," replied the deputy with a recalcitrant tone.

"Okay, how about Detective Brooks?"

"Yeah. The detective's here. Does he know what this is about?" replied the deputy.

"Just get him!" roared the red-faced FBI agent.

There was barely enough room in the office for Detective Brooks, much less the three visitors. "Whadya want?" he asked.

"I'd like to get some bottles of luminol from you," said Tim. "It has to do with the Coleman murder."

"Don't know what you need luminol for. I got the murderer back in my holdin' cell."

"Detective, I am aware that you have Billy Reese in your cells. I believe that we might have located a murder weapon, and I'd like the luminol to check it out."

"What're you doin' messing around in my investigation?" demanded Brooks.

"Well, detective, I didn't think you'd mind some low-key help. We certainly aren't trying to get in your way or steal any of the glory," said Tim.

"Ya ain't got no right to be sticking your nose in this. It's my investigation and my collar. So you c'n just butt out."

Tim kept smiling blandly. "I'm sorry you feel that way, detective. So, you feel you've got everything sewn up tight?"

"You're damn straight I do. S'cuse the language, Miss Paige."

"So you have the murder weapon?" asked Tim.

Brooks hesitated a moment. "No. I figures he tossed it inna water off the beach."

"Oh! So you figure the beach in Cape Charles is the crime scene?" queried Tim.

"'Course it is," replied Detective Brooks. "Where else? Why would Billy kill him somewheres else then haul him to the beach to hide the body?"

Tim just kept smiling mildly.

"So's I don't see why I need ta get you any luminol. It's open and shut."

Tim took a deep breath. *Here it comes,* thought Paige.

"Well, *detective.*" Tim said 'detective' as if tasting something particularly nasty. "I don't think that Coleman was killed on the beach at Cape Charles. And I don't think the murder weapon was tossed from the Cape Charles beach into The Bay."

Sneering, Brooks asked, "And just where do *you* think he got hisself killed?"

"I believe that Guy Coleman was murdered on the National Wildlife Refuge. NATIONAL Wildlife Refuge. That makes it my jurisdiction. Right? And I believe that we have the murder weapon, though I'm just a bit less certain of that."

Brooks sat there with his mouth hanging open.

"I don't yet have a solid on the motive for the murder, but I am reasonably certain that Billy Reese did not do it."

"Well, I ain't lettin' him outta jail without some better evidence than that," said Brooks.

"I'm not asking you to, at this time," said Tim. "Just be ready, though. Now, how about some luminol?"

"Well, Mr. G-man, if this is your case 'n jurisdiction, don't you think you oughta be using your official FBI investigatin' gear?"

Tim shook his head sadly. "I was hoping for a little professional courtesy, but I guess that was a hope misplaced. Thank you for your time, Detective," and he turned toward the door.

Brooks jumped to his feet. "Wait a minute, wait a minute," said Brooks. "Don't get your panties in a wad."

Spinning around and leaning over the desk, an artificially scandalized Paige said, "I beg your pardon?"

"Oh! Miss Paige! I'm so sorry for my language," said Brooks turning red and taking a hasty step back away from the desk.

Paige struggled to keep from laughing.

"I'll get you some luminol," said a chastened Brooks. "One bottle enough?"

"Make it three," said Tim.

"Yes. Of course. Wait here. I'll be right back."

As soon as Brooks had scurried out of the room Paige broke out with laughter.

"Shhh!" said Tim. "He's coming back."

With difficulty Paige composed herself.

Armed with the luminol they made a quick run to Yuk Yuk and Joe's for Billy's cheeseburger and then back out to Paige's apartment to feed Pongo and Ralph and wait for dark.

Neither Pongo nor Ralph were in forgiving moods after being left alone all day, and both let Paige know their displeasure. Ignoring Ralph, Pongo wrapped himself around Paige's ankles, threatening to trip her, and complained loudly about how put upon he was. It was bad enough to be left alone all day, but he could hear that bird scratching around inside its cage and smell it. And Ralph ... Ralph could hear Pongo stalking around outside his cage all day long. And the cat just wasn't any company at all.

At least that was how Paige anthropomorphized their loud complaints. Pongo was quickly mollified with a can of disgusting-looking and smelling gelatinous glop. Ralph, on the other hand, accepted the unsalted cashews he was offered but still threw the occasional one at Paige's head from his perch on her shoulder. He also muttered murderously, which was even more unnerving.

"What now?" asked Nott, urging the muttering Ralph onto his finger and then his shoulder.

"The luminescence from the blood is pretty dim, so we have to wait until dark," said Tim. "Once it is dark enough, we'll go on out to your house …"

"My shack, you mean."

"Well … yeah. We'll go out to your shack and spray each and every one of those stakes with the luminol. If there's even a trace of blood, we'll find it."

"Then what?"

"Well, if there's enough we can have the DNA compared with our victim's DNA. If not …"

Paige spoke up, "We can still pretty much make a case matching the stake to the wound on Coleman's head. Not as definitive as DNA, but still …"

Nott indicated his understanding.

"Then," said Tim, "we'll have the weapon, we'll be pretty certain of the venue, we've identified the victim … we'll just have to figure out 'why,' and then we can settle on our 'who.'"

"Who dun it," said Nott, grinning.

SINCE IT WAS October the sunset was at 6:24 pm, and they watched the lowering sun paint a vivid pink, purple, and blue pallet across the western sky as it dipped towards and then below the horizon.

"You know," said Nott, "seeing God do that always makes me feel like clapping."

Smiling her agreement, Paige said, "It is spectacular."

At the shack, they moored Nott's scow bow and stern below the pile of stakes.

"What we'll do," said Tim, "is each take a spray bottle and each start spraying stakes. If you see a faint blue glow, stop and call me over. Otherwise, after spraying the stake just toss it down into Nott's boat."

"Gotcha," said Paige. Nott just smiled and reached for a spray bottle.

The pile of stakes was large, and carefully spraying the luminol on all four sides took time. They worked silently for forty-five minutes until Nott said, "Whoa! Is this what we're looking for?"

Tim hurried over. Nott pointed to the discolored splotch on the wood and sprayed it again with the luminol. The spot glowed a ghostly blue.

"That's it," said Tim excitedly. "Nott, put that stake in your house to keep it separate while we check all the rest."

"You're going to check them all?" asked Paige. "We've got the one we were looking for."

"Yeah, but we want to make sure that it's the one. We don't want to find that someone cut their hand while pounding the stakes in and got blood on a bunch of them. We've got to eliminate all the others," responded Tim.

"Gotcha," she said as she picked up another stake and carefully sprayed it with the luminol.

"Poor Detective Brooks is gonna be flummoxed," said Nott, laughing softly.

Another hour passed before all the stakes had been checked. No other bloodstains were found.

"Looks like we've got a winner," said Tim.

"Can we fingerprint it to see who did it?"

"No, Nott. Wish we could. But even though the bloodstain was okay, the weather would have taken care of any fingerprints. Too bad, though. That would've been nice and definitive."

It was late and they were getting tired. Paige rubbed her eyes. "How about we all go back to Eastville and get some sleep? I need to take care of my animals, and I'm sure y'all are beat, too."

"Good idea," said Tim. "Then tomorrow we can go back to the Refuge and see how well our stake fits in one of those holes we found."

Twenty-two

THE NEXT MORNING Paige awoke to the tantalizing aromas of cafe con leche and warm croissants. Mentally praising a thoughtful Tim, she quickly dressed in pink sweatpants and a lightweight gray hoodie and went out into the living room.

Tim was sitting on the couch, drinking coffee in crisply-pressed bluejeans and an FBI polo shirt, and Nott was in the kitchen wearing the same clothes as yesterday. Ralph perched on Nott's shoulder, and the two of them were quietly having a bird-to-man conversation.

"Ol' Nott stopped by Machipongo Trading and brought us the coffees and croissants," said Tim.

Nott kind of hung his head, embarrassed by the attention. "I woke up real early, so I took the truck and drove out to Machipongo Trading. Got there before they even opened, so's I just sat in the dark waiting for them."

"You're a lifesaver," said Paige. "This cafe con leche is just what I needed to get going."

She smiled at Nott and Ralph. "Looks like you've made a friend, too."

Nott kind of grinned. "Yeah, well me 'n Ralph kind of hit it off. I don't talk much to people, you know, but he's real easy to talk to. Aren't you, buddy?"

"Awwrkk, Nott buddy. Nott buddy." Then he let loose with a white deposit on Nott's shoulder.

"There is that slight problem, though," said Nott. "He needs a cork or a diaper sometimes."

"Ralph is a dirty bird. Awwrkk. Dirty bird."

"That's okay, Ralph," said Nott. "You're still my buddy."

Ralph sidled closer to Nott's head and gently nibbled on his ear lobe. Nott giggled.

"Okay, people," said Paige, "what's on today's agenda?"

"Well, I bought an extra coffee and a breakfast burrito for Billy, so I'd like to warm them in the microwave and drop them off with him whenever we go somewhere."

"Nott!" said Paige. "That was so thoughtful. He'll appreciate them. I've seen some of what they call 'breakfast' in the jail."

Nott smiled, seeming pleased with himself.

Tim spoke up. "One of the first things I'd like to do is go pull Guy Coleman out of your cooler and compare the dent in the back of his head with our stake. And take some pictures. Then I'd like to go down to the Wildlife Refuge and see if it looks like the stake is one that made that hole. That'll give us a lot more in the way of direction."

Paige agreed. "Can you send the stake to your lab at Quantico to see if they can match the DNA to the victim's?"

"That's another good idea. I'll have to go across to my office to do that, but I guess I ought to check in, anyway."

"Yeah, I'm sure your Special Agent in Charge would appreciate that," laughed Paige.

"You don't need me for a while, I think I'll head back out to my house," said Nott. "Make sure it's still standing."

"Sounds like a plan to me." Tim tipped his cup to drain the last of his coffee and sighed contentedly. "Paige, we'll take Ralph with us this time. Let him get some fresh air."

"Why Special Agent Hannegan! I think you're getting soft for my parrot."

"Well, it looks like he's going to be around for a while, so I might as well try to make friends with him."

Paige retrieved Ralph from Nott's shoulder and slipped on his harness. Then they headed out the door. "Be good, Pongo," called Paige. "We'll be back for dinner."

As Paige stepped through the doorway, Ralph, sensing an opportunity, took flight.

"Damn it," she exclaimed. "I forgot to put his leash on with his harness."

As he flew they could hear Ralph — "Damn it! Damn it!"

Nott asked, "Will he come back?"

"Darned if I know."

They hurried outside where all three searched the sky for the escapee. "Oh, Ralph," moaned Paige. "Where'd you go?"

They suddenly heard an ungodly racket from the beach. They couldn't see what was happening because of the dunes. Paige raced toward the wooden walkway that crossed over the dunes when a green and gray apparition came streaking over the sand with a huge herring gull in hot and raucous pursuit. The green streak, which of course was Ralph, was screaming bloody murder and headed straight for Paige. This put the herring gull, with its four-foot wingspan and hard-as-nails beak, on a direct collision course with Paige's head.

She screamed, waving her hands. Fortunately, Ralph was more afraid of the gull than he was of Paige's attempt at dissuasion, and he flew to her shoulder, where he quickly burrowed into the depths of her hoodie.

Cursing loudly, in gullish, the gray-and-white herring gull peeled off and headed back to the beach.

Paige was shaking with fright, but Tim was shaking with laughter. "Yeah, Nott," he said, "I think he'll come back."

"Oh, ha, ha," said Paige. "Come on. Let's get Billy's breakfast to him and then get to work." In her temporary anger and angst, she sounded as severe as she could. It didn't stop Tim's laughter, much to her added anger. "Come … on," and she smiled slightly as she pulled Ralph out of her jacket, kissed him soothingly on the head, clipped on his leash, then let him burrow back into the dark.

When they arrived at the jail, Tim and Nott waited in the car while Paige took the coffee and burrito inside. Maddy was working the desk.

"Please send this back to Billy for his breakfast."

"Yes ma'am," said Maddy. She'd had her run-ins with Paige before and didn't want another one now, so she was very accommodating. Paige smiled at her grimly.

In Paige's workshop, they pulled Coleman's body from the cooler, and Tim and Nott transferred him onto a stainless-steel examination table. They placed him face-down so that the large depression on the back of his head was accessible. Paige turned on the powerful ceiling-mounted LED surgical exam light and pulled it close to the wound. To avoid any transfer, she first covered the wound with a thin membrane of surgical latex. Then taking the stake from Tim, she gently placed it in the impression. To the naked eye, it was a perfect fit.

"That's it," said Paige. "The stake fits the wound perfectly."

"Better and better," said Tim. "Now let's see if it fits the hole at the Refuge."

They slid the body back into the cooler and returned to the car. As they drove south on Lankford Highway Nott said, "Just drop me off at the wharf on your way down. I'll head back out to my house."

"You sure you don't want to go to lunch with us?" asked Paige.

Ralph broke into a chorus of,

♪♪ *Hit the road, Jack*
And don't you come back
No more, no more, no more, no more.

and then segued into,

♪♪ *Adios muchachos,*
Compañeros de mi vida!

Nott laughed. "I know when I'm not wanted. No, I've got to work my crab pots and take care of chores." Paige suspected that it was more that Nott was becoming overly saturated with people and needed to get back to his isolation and mental balance.

After dropping Nott off at his scow and waiting to make sure it started and didn't strand him at the dock, Tim and Paige drove on down to the National Wildlife Refuge. It seemed strange that just a few short weeks ago they had been down here bird watching and chatting with Old Miss Mary, and now they were back looking for evidence in a brutal murder. Life truly was strange.

Carrying the stake, they hiked to the bird watching blind, then beyond it to where they had found the hole. They slid the stake point-first into the small square hole, and it fit like a knife in a sheath.

"Getting more and more certain that this is the murder weapon," opined Tim. Tight-lipped, Paige smiled in agreement.

"As long as we're down here, let's go down to the Cove Beach Bar for lunch. We can check on Billy's boat, too," she said.

As they turned to walk out, they caught the aroma of rancid pipe tobacco. "Oh, no," said Paige, as Old Miss Mary emerged from the scrub.

She cast a rheumy eye on them. "What y'all doin' in ma Refuge?" she demanded. "You back in heyah nekkin'? Or maysbe you's smokin' some of that strange stuff? Hey?"

"Miss Mary, it's me ... Paige Reese. You know me."

Miss Mary said her name like she was tasting it, "Paige ... Reese. Yeah, I knows you gurl. But whatcha doin' back here in ma Refuge? And who's dis wit ya?"

"Miss Mary, this is Tim. You've met him before. Remember?"

"Hmmph. Maysbe I does and maysbe I don't." She cast an eye on the wooden stake Tim was carrying. "What that thin' fer?" she demanded. "Where'd you get 'at frum?" She suddenly looked at them with confused fear in her eyes. "Whatcha gonna do wit that big stick?" She looked around almost frantically. Her eyes widened. "Look over yonder!" she exclaimed pointing.

Tim and Paige quickly turned around to look where she was pointing. Nothing. When they turned back, Old Miss Mary was gone, melting back into the brush and scrub. The only thing that remained was the stench of her corn cob pipe.

"What the hell was that about?" asked Tim.

"I don't know," answered Paige. "I guess maybe she's lived out here by herself for too long." She started walking again. "Come on. Let's get some lunch and check on Billy's boat."

They ate fish cake sandwiches and drank Smith Island Oyster Stout, then went to check on Billy's boat, *Undertaker*.

"It's not locked!" exclaimed Paige after going aboard.

"We've been keepin' an eye on her," called Bill "Baloney" Cooper from several boats away. "Billy got them to let him lock up, but instead he jumped overboard and tried to escape. When they caught him they wouldn't let him come back and lock up so me and the rest of the boys been keeping watch on it. Make sure the kids don't get into it."

"Thank you so much," said Paige.

"How's Billy doin'?" asked Cooper. "He need anythin' up there?"

"No, thanks. Billy's fine. Baloney, you don't think he did it, do you?"

"No, honey. Billy ain't real bright, and he did get his clock cleaned by that guy after pickin' a fight with him, but, shoot, Billy ain't no murderer. Ain't got it in him."

"Thanks, Baloney," said Paige as she climbed off the boat and onto the floating dock.

"You make sure you tell him that we expect him back here real soon."

Paige waved back over her shoulder as she walked away.

Loudly Baloney called, "And tell him it's his turn to buy the beer," and he laughed until they were out of sight in the parking lot.

Twenty-three

IT WAS TIME to put the pieces of the puzzle together, see which parts were still missing, and analyze what they had found. Tim prided himself, while not being an investigative genius, on being excellent at finding all the pieces and arranging them to determine what was going on. He felt that he now had enough to make some headway.

Although he would have liked his entire Eastern Shore team together, Nott was out at his mid-creek shack. Tim would make do with just himself and Paige and Ralph. Paige wanted to do their analysis at Cape Charles Coffee House, but Tim didn't want the distractions there. They settled themselves around the coffee table in Paige's apartment. Keeping the screen slider closed, Paige cracked open the door out to the balcony to let in the fresh smells of the water and the beach. Ralph had already tried flying through the closed screen door and now knew not to try it again.

Through the cracked door they could hear the call of the laughing and herring gulls. These must have brought back bad memories for Ralph as he snuggled closer to Paige on her shoulder.

Tim took a yellow legal pad and a Mont Blanc pencil and started jotting notes.

"Let's see what we've got," he said. "Let's start with Coleman while he's still alive. He comes to town and checks in at the Hotel Cape Charles. We do not know who he contacted. Next, we have him sighted at the Eastern Shore National Wildlife Refuge with a group of unknown men, all of whom are dressed for business, not bird watching."

"Okay so far," said Paige.

"Next time we see Mr. Coleman he's dead, buried in the foot of a dune on Cape Charles beach."

Paige grimaced.

"We don't know who or how, but Nott, while scrounging ..."

"He thinks of it as 'shopping,'" Paige interjected.

"Nott, while 'shopping,' finds a large number of wooden engineer stakes on the sand at Pickett's Harbor, one of which seems to be the weapon which incapacitates Coleman, while not actually killing him. Blood is found on the stake with luminol, and we're waiting for Quantico to tell us whether or not it was Coleman's, but we are proceeding on the assumption that it is."

"Right ... Ow!"

Ralph had hopped onto Paige's arm and bit her, drawing a drop of blood.

"Why'd he do that?" asked Tim.

"Dumb bird! He sometimes thinks a mole or blemish is a seed and tries to pick it up to eat it. Don't you, you dumb bird?"

"Awwrkk! Dumb bird! Dumb bird.

♪♪ "Ay, ay, ay, ay,
    Canta y no llores,
    Porque cantando se alegran,
    cielitolindo, los corazones."

Tim laughed, and even Paige was forced to smile.

"Now, where was I? Oh, yeah. The stake. Okay, we 90% determined that the stakes came from the Refuge, based on the holes found and the fit of the stake and hole."

"What about the plastic?"

"Almost forgot. The holes in the Visqueen seem to match where Visqueen was fastened to the roof of the newly-constructed bird watching blind, which furthers our assumption that the murder took place on the Refuge."

"But, what do we have for motive?" asked Paige.

"I'm not sure. Let me think this out further. From the contents of his briefcase, we've determined that Coleman was in charge of obtaining land for the construction of wind farms. But there are no wind farms approved onshore down here."

"Thank goodness," murmured Paige.

"There is a wind farm approved, but that's twenty-seven miles offshore, and Coleman's company did not win the contract on that one."

Paige joined in. "We also know that even though Coleman's company is domiciled in Pensacola, Florida, it's owned by China. And China doesn't think twice about poaching things. Flat-out stealing, actually."

Tim took the topic back up. "So, let's theorize that China isn't happy losing the contract for building the several billion-dollar wind farm and isn't happy about losing the ongoing sale of wind-generated electricity to the grid. They decide to do something about it."

Paige took up the narrative. "So, they find an onshore location to build a competing wind farm. It'll be cheaper to build and maintain onshore, and cheaper to ship the electricity to the grid with tower-carried high-tension lines than with cables on the seabed."

Tim took over. "Because of the savings in construction, maintenance, and transmission the Chinese will be able to undercut the kilowatt cost of the electricity and outcompete the offshore farm."

Tim flopped back on the couch. "Wow! Do you think that's really what is happening?"

Paige pressed her lips together. "But Tim, all of that land is protected. You know, I saw stakes out on the barrier islands, too, but it's off-limits. There's nothing the Chinese can do about that."

"Paige, what about that group of businessmen Edd saw out there with Coleman?"

"What about them?"

"Just suppose," said Tim, "just suppose that those were the conservators of the properties. You know, the bureaucrats from the United States Fish and Wildlife Service and directors from The Nature Conservancy. Now, if Coleman can convince them that the wind farm isn't going to spoil the land, just a bunch of towers, nothing destructive, and sweeten the deal with over or under-the-counter donations ..."

"You mean bribes?"

"Well, not necessarily. The Nature Conservancy operates on donations. And the Fish and Wildlife Service ... well, yeah, I guess maybe their *inducements* might be a little more direct."

Paige thought about it for a moment. "Yeah. I can see that happening. China can't get it the honest way, so they go ahead through the back door. All it takes is some money to grease some palms. Smart. Crooked as a snake with colic, but smart."

"A snake with colic?" Tim smiled.

"You know what I mean. But what got Coleman killed? And who killed him? And since the stake to the head didn't do it, how was he killed? For that matter, where's Jimmy Hoffa's body?"

"Jimmy Hoffa what?" exclaimed Tim.

Paige chuckled. "I just wanted to make sure you were still with me."

Tim smiled ruefully. "I didn't say I had it *all* worked out. But we're a lot further along than we were."

Paige walked over and looked out the slider. "The tide's out and the sun's warm, let's go take a walk on the beach and let all of this simmer."

"Okay," said Tim.

Paige put a much-protesting Ralph in his cage and threw a cover over it to calm him down. Then she closed and locked the balcony door. "We'll be back soon," she called to Ralph and Pongo as they went out the door.

Down on the beach, they turned south and after a short while they were walking through the Savage Neck Dunes Natural Area Preserve. The beach was absolutely deserted with nothing but silver-bleached driftwood adorning the sand.

"When I was in high school, we used to come down here to neck."

"Really? Tell me more," grinned Tim.

Paige started to turn red. "No. I just … I thought I'd mention it. It's been deserted like this forever."

"I kinda guessed that's why they named it a 'natural area preserve'," said Tim.

Paige's blush grew a little more intense.

"Just where did this nefarious necking activity take place?" asked Tim.

"I wish I hadn't mentioned it at all!" said Paige, and stalked on ahead. She could hear Tim's quiet laughter follow her.

Tim was down near the water. "Hey, Paige," he called. "What's this thing?"

He was standing over what looked like a shiny brown armored tank with a long pointy tail.

"That's a horseshoe crab," said Paige, walking over.

"A crab?" he asked. "Is it edible?"

"I'm sure somewhere some people eat them, but no, we don't. They're interesting, though. They breed up in the Delaware Bay. Thousands of them each spring."

"Just there?"

"On the Atlantic Coast, yes. And they are valuable medically."

"Medically?"

"Yeah. They have blue blood and it is used for lots of different medical things."

"Live and learn," said Tim, shaking his head.

"Like I said, Yankee. Stick with this ol' country gal and I'll larn ya some things."

Tim adopted as southern a drawl as he could, "Well, I 'on't plans on leavin' ya anytimes soon, ma'am."

Paige reached out and took his hand, and they continued their walk. Soon, though, the driftwood got so thick that they couldn't go any further, and they turned back for Paige's apartment.

They took off their sandy shoes before going in.

"I'm cold, now," said Paige. "You want some coffee?"

Paige went to the refrigerator and pulled out a large pitcher of coffee. She poured out two mugs and put them in the microwave.

Oh, no, thought Tim. *Leftover coffee. This's gonna be brutal.*

Paige handed Tim a steaming mug, then waited and watched.

He smiled at her, braced himself, and took a sip.

"Wow! That's pretty good," he exclaimed.

Paige laughed. "I was waiting to see your reaction. Thought it was leftover, huh?"

He nodded his head.

"Cold-brewed. As a matter of fact, it's blended just for cold brewing. Right here in Eastville!"

"Really?"

"Yup. Eastern Shore Coastal Roasting. And that coffee you're drinking is called Marsh Mud Cold Roast."

"Marsh Mud? Like that smell I get when I hit Fisherman's Island and the tide's out?"

Paige laughed. "Yeah, and you can just about get those piquant undertastes when you sip it gently."

"Damn, girl," exclaimed Tim.

"Awwrkk, damn it! Damn it!" came muffled from the covered cage in the corner.

Twenty-four

PAIGE PUT HER coffee cup down on the table. "So, who would benefit from Coleman's death?" she asked. "If he were bribing the bureaucrats to let them build a wind farm in the Refuge, wouldn't killing him be killing the golden goose?"

Tim raised his eyebrows. "Maybe one of them got religion and realized that he was violating his oath. He got remorseful, but Coleman wouldn't let him off the hook. So, the bribee killed the briber."

"You think?" asked Paige, a thoughtful look on her face. She stood and took their empty coffee cups to the kitchen sink.

"Well," said Tim, "some people are terribly protective of their reputations. Especially if that's all they have. So, I think it's possible. I just don't know who the suspects are to judge if it's probable."

Paige stopped washing the cups and turned. "How can we figure out who the people were with Coleman in the Refuge?"

"Let's check with the hotel to see if he made any calls. And I'll have my office run his cell phone to see what numbers he called. That might give us an idea. But I'm still not too hopeful."

Paige went back to the living room and took her seat on the sofa. "Okay, let's look at this rationally," she said. "You know the FBI's data on murder. What are the most prevalent causes of murder?"

"Robbery, sex, or vengeance."

"What else?"

"Murders are committed by ten times more men than women. And the vast majority of murders are men murdered by someone they don't know."

"Really?" Paige raised her eyebrows in surprise. "I thought the majority were men killed by their wives."

"No, you've been watching too many cop shows on television. That's just what the popular culture wants you to think."

"Okay, then, we have a male victim. He's not killed for a domestic problem, so that probably rules out sex. His Rolex and wallet were left behind, so that rules out robbery. Vengeance? How could revenge play into this? For revenge you have to know someone, don't you?"

"Yeah, I guess so," responded Tim. "I mean, it's hard to want revenge on someone you don't know. Revenge is a reaction, yes?"

"So what does that leave us?"

"Leaves me with a headache," said Tim. "I just don't know."

Paige yawned hugely. "Tell you what," she said, "let's sleep on it, let it ferment in our minds, and tomorrow we can get

Nott, go back to the Refuge, and do another thorough search for ... well, for anything we missed the first time."

"Sounds good to me," said Tim. He stood, gave Paige a quick hug, and said, "Come on Pongo. Let's call it a night." He headed into the guest room.

Poor Ralph had been in his cage for most of the day. Paige took him out and into her bedroom while she prepared for bed.

Ralph enjoyed being with Paige, and loved flying around her large bedroom, picking up shiny trinkets and dropping them where they didn't belong. He also liked to get into the sink while Paige was running the water to brush her teeth. He'd duck his head under the water, then shake and fluff his feathers, preening.

When Paige stepped into the shower, Ralph wanted to join her, but Paige put a stop to that. "Ralph, the water's too strong and too hot. I'm afraid you'd hurt yourself."

"Awwrkk, Ralph is a dirty bird. Dirty bird! Dirty bird!"

"Maybe so, but your head is all that's getting wet tonight. It'll take too long to bathe you and get you dry so you don't catch your death. You're a pain in the neck, but I'd miss you if you weren't here."

Ralph started singing a new one:

♪♪ *"It's the yellow rose of Texas*
That I am going to see ..."

"Come on, Tex. It's time to go back to your corral for the night," and Paige tucked Ralph back into his cage and pulled the cover closed. "Good night, bird."

THE NEXT MORNING neither Paige nor Tim felt like cooking. They drove down to Cape Charles, hoping to catch Nott "shopping" amidst the jetsam on the beach. Fortunately, he was.

"Hey, Nott," called Tim. "How about some breakfast at Rayfield's?"

Nott waved happily. He loved nothing better than a big country breakfast cooked up by Birdie, the perennially good-natured cook cum counterman cum clerk at Rayfield's Pharmacy. He especially liked it when someone else was paying.

"Shur is good to see y'all," said Birdie as she served up their breakfasts. "Nott, I ain't never seen you lookin' so good. Miss Paige, you've done a wonder with him."

Birdie was a scrawny, tall, gray-haired old woman of indeterminate age. Before Paige had taken Nott under her wing, Birdie was often the only person in the county who cared for him. Nott would drop Rayfield's for coffee every morning, and when she could, Birdie would slip him a complete hearty breakfast. She knew Nott's story and had love and respect for any wounded veteran.

They sat up to the brick-fronted counter and ate their eggs and grits and bacon and biscuits with thick-sausage gravy and discussed what they wanted to accomplish at the Refuge.

"So, what are we looking for?" asked Nott.

"That's just it," said Tim, swiping a piece of biscuit through his gravy.. "I don't know. Won't know until we see it. Anything that … well, anything that seems important." He popped the bite in his mouth and closed his eyes at the sudden influx of heavenly flavors.

"It'd be nice to find a hand-lettered sign that says, 'It Happened Here,'" said Paige, "but I'm not counting on it." She stirred more cream in her coffee.

"You know how it is," said Tim. "Every time you go through somewhere you see things differently. We're just banking on seeing something different that is significant this time."

"Yeah, okay," said Nott, around a mouthful of eggs. "How about running me back by my boat? I've got one of those big stakes. I can use it to poke around in the brush."

"Sure," said Tim as he laid down payment for their breakfasts and a large gratuity.

"Y'all come back soon," called Birdie and waved as they went out the door.

"She's always been real nice to me," said Nott. "She'd take care of me back when I was … well, screwed up."

Paige smiled, remembering.

It was a bright and crisp morning when they got to the Wildlife Refuge. There were a number of bird watchers just wandering with binoculars hanging around their necks while others sat in the blinds.

"We've got to be careful," said Paige. "This is prime migration time for these birds and we don't want to stir up trouble. Just watch where you step, and try not to make a lot of fuss."

"We'll go off separately," said Tim. "That way there should be less fuss and we can cover more ground."

They all agreed and headed out from their parked car. Fortunately, they had all brought sunglasses because the rising sun was very bright.

They were soon out of sight of one another, each concentrating on what was just before and around them and not concerned with what the others were doing.

As Nott poked around with his stake there came a sudden shaking of the brush to his left and the unmistakable stench of a corn cob pipe smoking a truly fetid tobacco. At least he thought it might be tobacco.

"You!" Old Miss Mary yelled as she came out of the brush. "Thief! Stop, thief!"

"Hey, Miss Mary, how're you today?"

"Thief! Wat yadoin' stealin' an ol' woman's warmth? Thief!"

"What are you talking about, Miss Mary? I'm not stealing anything."

"Right thar in yor hand! Thief. Ma fahrwood! How's I s'posed to keep warm y'all steals ma fahrwood?"

Nott was perplexed. "Miss Mary, I don't know what you're talkin' about."

"How c'nya stands thar holdin' a stob in yer hand and tell me ya don't know what I'm talkin' 'bout? Yerstealin' ma fahrwood!"

"You mean this stake?" asked Nott, holding up the piece of wood.

"'At's mine," spit the old woman. "Ah had me a whole bunch of it on me porch, an' you done stole it. Thief! How'm I s'posed ta cook and stay warm if'n some swamp rat steals ma fahrwood?" She yelled at the top of her lungs, "Hep me! Thief!"

All of the noise brought Tim and Paige running.

"Hi, Miss Mary," said Paige.

"Who're you?" demanded the old woman.

"You know me, Miss Mary. I'm Paige Reese from up to Eastville."

"I'on't know no Paige."

"Sure you do. Remember, we saw you just a few days ago?"

The old woman just grumbled under her breath. "You friends wit' dis fahrwood thief? See? He gots a stick of it right thar."

"He didn't steal that, Miss Mary. Nott found that stake on the sand over at Pickett's Harbor. What makes you think it's yours?"

"I knows 'tis. I had big pile of 'em sticks on th' porch ta ma shack 'n now alls gone. If'n him didn' steal 'em whar'd they go?"

Tim spoke up, "A whole bunch of stakes?"

She nodded.

"Just like that one that Nott's holding now?"

She nodded again.

"Miss Mary," asked Tim gently, "where did all those stakes come from?"

Suddenly Old Miss Mary took on a wary look. "I found 'em."

Paige spoke up. "Where did you find them, Miss Mary?"

Old Miss Mary was now looking a bit like a cornered animal. She glanced around fitfully.

"I found 'em. They's mine. An' he stole 'em."

"Were they sticking up from the ground here, in the Refuge, and you pulled them up?"

"My Refuge, my fahrwood."

Paige looked at Tim and Nott. "She found the stakes that Guy Coleman laid out here to mark the proposed wind farm and pulled them up."

Nott said, "Heck, nothing wrong with that. They're the ones that were committing the crime."

"Is that what happened, Miss Mary? You found them sticking up from the ground in your Refuge so you pulled them up and stacked them on your porch to use as stove wood?"

"Hmmph. My Refuge, my wood. C'ain't nobody take it from me."

"Miss Mary, the man who had put all those stakes out, did he come to your shack?"

"Nasty man! Yelled at me somethin' fierce. Shook his fist right in ma face! Went on 'bout the hours he'd spent poundin' those stakes. Turned real red-faced. Used words on me! Cursed!"

"What happened then, Miss Mary," Paige urged gently.

"He cursed me, Miss Paige! Used such foul words! Just 'bout then my boy Edd came by wit' some fresh caught fish for me. Nasty man turned 'round to Edd's truck an' I hit him right solid wit' one dem stakes."

"You hit him in the back of the head?" asked Tim.

"Yessir. I fetched him a good one. Teach him to curse an old lady."

"Miss Mary, what happened next?" asked Paige.

"Well, man he felled to ground jest screamin' and carryin' on. My Edd had him a basket a fresh caught fish. He took one of those spiny blowfish and shoved it in'a man's mout to shut him up. An' ya know what? Guess dat fish didn' like the yellin' neither 'cause he puffed hisself up full of air and kind a shut the man up. Man tried pullin' da fish out, but dem blowfish, they gets scared they jest blow up like pork-o-pine balloon an' he couldn' budge him." The old lady laughed and laughed. "He looked so funny wit' that fish tail stickin' outta his mout."

"Then what?" asked Tim.

"Man he fell down on ground and flopped around like *he* was a fish. When he stopped, my Edd went and got a piece a plastic to wrop him in. Then Edd took him away."

Miss Mary smiled with the memory. "Hmmph. Ain't thought 'bout that for longest time. Wonder what ever become o' dat man?"

Twenty-five

IT TOOK A lot of convincing for Detective Brooks to accept that the perpetrator he presently had sitting in his holding cell, Billy Reese, was, in fact, completely innocent of the crime. He had been so sure and was so proud of his apprehension of the suspect. In fact, if it weren't for Tim's threat to bring in the Bureau and wrench the entire investigation away from the Northampton County Sheriff's Department, Billy would probably still be in jail. Or possibly prison.

Tim's pressure had forced Detective Brooks to go and arrest Edd Collins at his home, and then go collect Old Miss Mary, too. He was more afraid of arresting the old lady than her great-grandson, but he took a young deputy with him, ostensibly as training for the young officer. He managed it, though his ears took a beating.

On the way back to the sheriff's office, Old Miss Mary kept up a constant barrage of invective against "no 'count ruffians what would treat an old lady thus." She poured some of her condemnation on poor Edd for not sticking up for his "sick and helpless ol' granny." She muttered curses and imprecations directed at Detective Brooks, who sat hunched down in his seat trying to become invisible. He'd heard that the old woman was a witch and conjured evil. Although he didn't believe in such, he still worried.

For his part, Edd just cried piteously all the way back. When they got to the jail and got him processed in Edd was softened up enough that he gave a complete confession. He told how he had arrived at Old Miss Mary's shack just in time to see her take a stake from the porch of her house and slam it down on the back of the head of the stranger when he turned away from the old woman to look at Edd's arrival.

The man had fallen to the ground like a pole-axed steer and began yelling and blathering about getting the law and locking them both up for the rest of their lives. Edd tried to calm the man and reason with him, but when the man kept yelling at the top of his voice, Edd grabbed a fish from the peach basket-full he had brought for his grandmother and shoved it in the man's mouth. Unfortunately for Coleman, the fish was a very freshly-caught spiny blowfish who, in response to this added insult, immediately puffed up to his fully-inflated state. His spines lodged in the tender tissues of Coleman's mouth, resisting any attempt to pull him out. He also created a form-fitting plug, efficiently closing off the yelling, and, concurrently, the breathing.

When Coleman finally stopped flopping around, Edd took his fillet knife and punctured the bladder of the puffer allowing for its removal. He then drove over to the newly-constructed bird-watching blind and tore the Visqueen from its roof. He returned to the shack, wrapped Coleman in the plastic, and put him in the back of his truck.

Edd then took his great-grandmother inside the shack and lit a small fire in her wood stove to take off the chill. He fried up some of the fish for the old lady and then, with a kiss on her forehead, put her to bed.

Going back outside, Edd took the accusatory stakes off the porch and put them in the back of the truck with the body. He first drove to Pickett's Harbor where he dumped the stakes on the beach, figuring the winter storms would wash them away. He then drove to Cape Charles. By now it was pitch dark and after midnight. It was cold and the beach was deserted. Edd took the body over the dunes to the bayside and buried it in the sand. He had removed the man's watch and wallet before wrapping him in the plastic, thinking that maybe he could pawn the watch. But now he was feeling so sick at what he'd done that he simply buried the watch and the wallet further down the beach. Maybe when they weren't found on the body the police would think it was a robbery and go off in the wrong direction with their investigation.

Edd never mentioned what had happened to Old Miss Mary, and she conveniently forgot all about it. Even after the body turned up, Edd felt that he was safe. There was no way anybody could connect him or his great-grandma to the man or to his death. It was unfortunate that it had happened, but she was a decrepit old woman whose mind was kinda slippin'. Who could possibly pin this on her? Who, indeed.

Once he had the confession in hand, Detective Brooks was forced to release Billy. He was embarrassed and not gracious about it, but when Billy demanded that the Sheriff's Department transport him back to his boat he was warned not to push his luck. "You mighta ducked this one," Brooks told him, "but I'm sure if we look hard enough we can find something to charge you with." Not willing to risk it, Billy called Paige who picked him up and drove him back to Mallard Cove. He got there just in time for the convening of the Beer-Thirty Group and was able to use his story to cage free beers for the rest of the night.

After dropping Billy off, Paige and Tim went to Jackspots. They never had gotten to finish their Bloody Marys, but it was too late in the day for them now, and the "Mary" was an unwelcome reminder. They were bundled warmly, so they each got a Smith Island Oyster Stout and parked themselves out on the patio. They just sat there, not discussing the case or the weather or anything as they waited for the sunset.

And from his spot, warm within Paige's jacket snuggled to her side, Ralph snored contentedly.

Epilogue

THE TRIAL DIDN'T take too long. Edd Collins, Old Miss Mary's great-grandson, was convicted by a jury of his peers for the voluntary manslaughter of Guy Coleman. He was sentenced to ten years' incarceration in Red Onion State Prison in Pound, Virginia, where he remains today.

At trial, Old Miss Mary Collins was found to be *non compos mentis*. She spent three months at the Central State Hospital in St. Petersburg, Virginia, and was then released to go back to her ramshackle home in the National Wildlife Refuge. She spends her time rocking on her front porch, watching the hummingbirds come to the feeders that some nice boy (actually her great-grandson Edd) hung for her. She sometimes wonders who the nice boy was and why he hasn't come back to visit her, but she is unable to maintain that train of thought long while her colorful beauties are flitting around the feeders. She does have that nice young couple from "up the way" stop by with an occasional casserole. What she longs for is a nice pan of fried blowfish.

Finally, the Federal Fish and Wildlife Service and The Nature Conservancy have purged themselves of as many of those they could find who were willing to despoil these wilderness areas for the sake of Chinese dollars. While the offshore wind farm continues on, it will be a long time before such a thing is tried again in a protected area.

The Law of Unintended consequences

WIND TURBINE BLADES FILLING UP LANDFILLS

BY WAYNE CREED,
CAPE CHARLES MIRROR

WIND TURBINE'S BLADES at the end of their lifespan must be sawed through using a diamond-encrusted industrial saw to create pieces small enough to be strapped to a tractor-trailer.

The municipal landfill in Casper, Wyoming, is the final resting place of 870 blades whose days making renewable energy have come to end.

Tens of thousands of aging blades are ending up in landfills. In the U.S. alone, about 8,000 will be removed in each of the next four years. Europe, which has been dealing with the problem longer, has about 3,800 coming down annually through at least 2022.

Built to withstand extremely high winds, the blades can't easily be crushed, recycled or repurposed. Only landfills in Lake

Mills, Iowa; Sioux Falls, South Dakota; and Casper, where they will be in stacks that reach 30 feet underground.

GREEN ENERGY'S DIRTY SECRETS

BY WAYNE CREED,
CAPE CHARLES MIRROR

THE ENERGY FROM sunshine and wind is obviously clean, however, the infrastructure we need to capture it is not. The transition to renewables is going to require a dramatic increase in the extraction of metals and rare-earth minerals.

The ecological and social costs associated with this work is real.

In 2017, the World Bank released a little-noticed report that offered the first comprehensive look at this question. It models the increase in material extraction that would be required to build enough solar and wind utilities to produce an annual output of about 7 terawatts of electricity by 2050.

Using wind, solar, and energy storage batteries as proxies, the study examines which metals will likely rise in demand to be able to deliver on a carbon-constrained future. Metals which could see a growing market include aluminum (including its key constituent, bauxite), cobalt, copper, iron ore, lead, lithium, nickel, manganese, the platinum group of metals, rare earth metals including cadmium, molybdenum, neodymium, and indium—silver, steel, titanium and zinc. The report then maps production and reserve levels of relevant metals globally, focusing on implications for resource-rich developing countries.

By doubling the World Bank figures, we can estimate what it will take to get all the way to zero emissions: 34 million metric tons of copper, 40 million tons of lead, 50 million tons of zinc, 162 million tons of aluminum, and no less than 4.8 billion tons of iron.

As the world goes crazy trying to replace fossil fuels with clean energy, the environmental impact of finding all the lithium required to enable that transformation could become a serious issue in its own right. One of the biggest environmental problems caused by our endless hunger for the latest and smartest devices is a growing mineral crisis, particularly those needed to make our batteries.

In South America, the biggest problem is water. The continent's Lithium Triangle, which covers parts of Argentina, Bolivia and Chile, holds more than half the world's supply of the metal beneath its salt flats. It's also one of the driest places on earth. To extract lithium, miners start by drilling a hole in the salt flats and pumping salty, mineral-rich brine to the surface.

Then they leave it to evaporate for months at a time, first creating a mixture of manganese, potassium, borax and lithium salts which is then filtered and placed into another evaporation pool. After between 12 and 18 months, the mixture has been filtered enough that lithium carbonate can be extracted.

The process uses approximately 500,000 gallons of water per tonne of lithium. In Chile's Salar de Atacama, mining activities consumed 65 per cent of the region's water, which impacts local farmers—who grow quinoa and herd llamas—in an area where some communities already have to get water driven in from elsewhere.

Toxic chemicals also leak from the evaporation pools into the water supply. These include chemicals, including hydrochloric acid, which are used in the processing of lithium into a form that can be sold, as well as those waste products that are filtered out of the brine at each stage. In Australia and North America, lithium is mined from rock using more traditional methods, but still requires the use of chemicals in order to extract it in a useful form. Research in Nevada found impacts on fish as far as 150 miles downstream from a lithium processing operation.

Like any mining process, lithium mining is invasive, it scars the landscape, it destroys the water table and it pollutes the earth and the local wells. Is this really a green solution?

According to a report by Friends of the Earth, lithium extraction inevitably harms the soil and causes air contamination. In Argentina's Salar de Hombre Muerto, locals claim that lithium operations have contaminated streams used by humans and livestock, and for crop irrigation. In Chile, there have been clashes between mining companies and local communities, who say that lithium mining is leaving the landscape marred by mountains of discarded salt and canals filled with contaminated water with an unnatural blue hue.

Cobalt and nickel, also used in electric vehicles, offer a potentially huge environmental cost. Cobalt is found in huge quantities right across the Democratic Republic of Congo and central Africa, and hardly anywhere else. The price has quadrupled in the last two years.

Unlike most metals, which are not toxic when they're pulled from the ground as metal ores, cobalt can be poisonous in excessive doses.

The Congo is home to 'artisanal mines', where cobalt is extracted from the ground by hand, often using child labour, without protective equipment.

Acknowledgments

I NEED TO thank Don Rich (the COASTAL ADVEN-TURE series) and Michael Reisig (the ROAD TO KEY WEST series), two of my favorite authors, who convinced me to keep writing. David Thatcher Wilson, whose Demon Series book THE EXQUISITE CORPSE gave me my main character, Paige Reese, fully developed. The Cape Charles Coffee House exists and is a delightful spot in downtown Cape Charles. They are in a beautifully restored bank building. You really should check out their website at https://www.capecharlescoffeehouse.com/. Also look into brown dog ice cream, http://http://www.brown-dogicecream.com/

On the highway across the street from the Barrier Island Center, is Machipongo Trading Company (http://www.esvamtc.com/), another wonderful spot for coffee, sandwiches, soups, and sundries.

And as improbable as it sounds, Yuk Yuk and Joe's is a popular watering hole in Eastville. Looks like a dive from the outside, but inside you'll find warm Shore courtesy and great fresh seafood.

I'd also like to give credit to DonRichBooks.com and Florida Refugee Press, LLC of the Coastal Adventure Series of books for use of Mallard Cove Marina™, The Cove Beach Bar™, and The Cove Restaurant™.

If you found RALPH fascinating and now want to purchase a Quaker Parrot for a pet, I need to tell you a couple of things:

First, I don't have one. I don't know anyone who has one. The only thing I know about Quaker Parrots is what I've read online, and that's mixed.

Second, owning Quaker Parrots is illegal in several states. They are considered an invasive species.

Finally, they live up to twenty years! If you get one for a pet, you are in it for the long haul. Twenty years! You'd better be darn sure you want one of these for a pet.

In closing, I'd like to offer an apology to my Eastern Shore brethren. For the sake of the story, I had to take the occasional license with some of the facts and locations. You'll catch them, though anyone not familiar with The Shore shouldn't even notice.

Philosophical Reflections On Shorebirds

HAVE YOU EVER considered a comparative study of bird flight? No, really! Sitting here, at the beach, I've had an opportunity to indulge myself in some deep philosophical reflections, one of which has been the flight characteristics of birds relative to species and assumed psycho/social proclivities. I find that it is a very underrated yet intellectually stimulating field of study.

Contemplate the following: Seagulls tend to be scavengers. Whenever possible they do not do their own foraging for food ... they eat whatever garbage they can find wherever they happen to find it. Of course, they are pretty egalitarian. Once they find a source for a free meal they call all of their buddies to join in. [They are a lot like charities in that way. Once you give to one, hundreds seem to come out of the woodwork looking for handouts.] But essentially seagulls are lazy. They are very laid back, and their flight patterns reflect it. They fly with a very economical wing movement. A little up, a little down, and if there is a wind, coast as much as possible. They always seem to be going somewhere, but there is little agreement on where that is. Some are heading this way while others are heading that. No seeming rhyme or reason.

The Brown Pelicans, on the other hand, all seem to know just where they are headed. There is usually a string of five-or-so of them, gracefully skimming just at wave top height. Very self-assured. It seems you seldom see them move their wings at all ... almost as though they have a built-in tailwind keeping them aloft. Stately. They don't really care what other fowl are up to. Indeed, it seems beneath them to even consider the question. Of course their veneer of elegance is rudely ripped away when they come in for a landing. Then their aerodynamic properties change from glider to bowling ball as they crash into the water with all of the grace and beauty of a pregnant warthog. Pseudo-sophisticates.

Pigeons are the real obsessive-compulsives. They fly so hard that you can hear their wings slapping together! It's almost as though they have a built-in headwind that they constantly must fight. And they simply cannot fly off on their own. Paranoically, they are always afraid that some other Pigeon is going to get something they aren't. That's why you always see them flying in large flocks and always changing directions. "Hey, where's that guy going?" And they all swoop off in that direction. "Wait a minute ... look where he is headed!" And they all fly off after him. Neurotics! Every one of them.

Sandpipers don't fly too much. They are the maiden aunts of the bird world. Sandpipers bustle around the sand, sticking their nose [well, bill] in here and then in there, and then following the water as it goes out, AND THEN RUNNING LIKE CRAZY AS IT COMES BACK IN. [You'd think they'd learn the trick, but they keep wandering out as the waves retreat, AND THEN FRANTICALLY RUNNING TO KEEP THEIR FEET DRY. Not smart.]

Then there is the solitary Osprey. Don't even think about messing with him. He slowly, regally, beats the air with his wings, soaring up in the sky, until … suddenly … HEFOLD-SHISWINGSANDDIVESINTOTHEWATERBEFOREYOU-CANBLINK! Then he shakes off the water and the bonds of the earth and fights his way skyward with slow, powerful strokes as he carries his catch back to the nest. Self-sufficient. Autonomous. Stately. Imperious. Introverted overachievers?

I guess the Canada Geese are the Jewish mothers. The yentas. They all cluster around in one big crowd, and then they take off en masse, with such a honking and talking and carrying on … sounds like a Hadassah meeting when the refreshments have run out. Everyone talking, no one listening, oy!

There is a bird over here called the Black Skimmer. I guess he is the teenager of the crowd. He has a terrible underbite (the only bird whose lower mandible is longer than his upper), which might be the reason for his show-offy behavior. He spends his day, usually with a date, flying at breakneck speed, skimming through the shallows with his bottom lip [well, bill] dragging in the water. Kind of like a perpetual pout. I KNOW his mother must have told him, "If you keep doing that your face will freeze like that." Just another adenoidal mouth-breather trying to be cool. I can't help but wonder what would happen if that lower lip hooked a good-sized fish. Another teenager hoisted on his own petard.

I remember watching the swallows that nested under the wharf up in Maine. They were like hyperactive children who had forgotten to take their Ritalin®. Good grief! Swooping and darting and diving, here and there and back again! You just know that somewhere there is a mother swallow, feathers gray and ragged, looking for a government program to narcotize her frenetic children before she flips out completely … Ritalin® for them, Prozac® for her.

Then, of course, there is the neighborhood intimidator. Come on, you know who I mean. That's right, the nockingbird. Sits up on the peak of the roof, chest puffed out, telling everyone about how cool he is. Then when the poor dog wanders out to take a leak, old Mockingbird pops up, locks his wings in attack mode, and dive-bombs the heck out of her. Pecks her head and her rear, when all she is doing is looking for the proper place to poop. He thinks he's so cool. He better remember that "It's a sin to kill a mockingbird" will only take you so far. Bully.

You see? Calm reflections by the soothing water of The Chesapeake Bay can lead to truly seminal philosophical discoveries on the nature of life and living things. Or do you think I've been out of touch for a touch too long?

Cherrystone Creek

Mysteries

LITTLE GIRL UNKNOWN
(The Cherrystone Creek Mysteries Book 1)

HTTPS://TINYURL.COM/YCU9A2R6

SOUTHERN BORN AND bred, Paige Reese plans to escape the stagnant Eastern Shore of Virginia for a big city career. When Paige's daddy dies unexpectedly, she agrees to return home to take care of his funeral business. As the acting coroner and mortician for small town Eastville, Paige has plenty of time to resent her new life while trying to force a pleasant outlook for the locals.

Iraqi-war veteran Nott Smith has deeper scars than his fractured legs admit. Battling severe PTSD keeps Nott busy as he drifts around Cape Charles, collecting and restoring remnants of trash. Always a loner, Nott prefers to let his demons rage silently than to make friends in the quaint bay-side town. Good thing for Nott, Paige isn't asking to be his friend.

When the unidentified body of a migrant girl is discovered in Cherrystone Creek near Nott's ramshackle house and the Chief Deputy arrests Nott for the murder, Paige acts on instinct. Her new friend couldn't be guilty of the crime. Could he?

With more questions than answers, Paige works to uncover the victim's identity and cause of death, who is responsible, and why the authorities aren't pursuing the murderer. Then the truth confronts Paige with the ugly possibility that her closest friends are more involved than she realized. Can she avoid becoming the next victim?

BREAKWATER SKELETON UNKNOWN
(Cherrystone Creek Mysteries Book 2)

HTTPS://TINYURL.COM/Y9H2WE8E

MAKING DRY BONES talk is Paige Reese's specialty.

After the untimely death of her close friend, Paige wants only one thing: to become better acquainted with FBI Special Agent Tim Hannegan. AKA: Agent Dish. Unfortunately, Paige has other work to do.

As Coroner Ad Hoc for the small bayside community of Northampton County on Virginia's Eastern Shore, she sees every deadbeat in town. So, when the Coast Guard locates the sun-bleached bones of a skeleton on a nearby breakwater ship Paige makes it her business to determine the identity of the deceased. She has few clues to go on. What do a dismembered skeleton, white fishing boots, and a saint's medallion all have in common?

Nott Smith lends an investigative hand, and Paige begins sorting out the puzzle of the unknown. Then a warning note arrives, urging Paige to let the dead rest in peace. If she doesn't obey, it could be her own dry bones telling the story.

With colorful descriptions of Virginia's beautiful Eastern Shore and her unique community of locals, BREAKWATER SKELETON UNKNOWN is the second installment in the Cherrystone Creek Mystery series. Don't miss the first book in the series, LITTLE GIRL UNKNOWN, which introduces Paige, Nott, and Tim, as well as their scenic—and mysterious—fishing town. Get hooked today!

PRAISE FOR LITTLE GIRL UNKNOWN:

"A really great mystery" with *"real characters that truly caught my attention,"* best-selling author Michael Reisig calls Emma Jackson *"an author to watch... and read."*

"A thrilling mystery." Pat Wise, reader

"Definitely worth the read!" Haley Goffigon Smith, reader

"An Eastern Shore gem!" Don Rich, author of the Coastal Adventure series

Learn more about Paige in
THE EXQUISITE CORPSE,
available on Amazon.

Learn more about the Eastern Shore in AN EASTERN
SHORE SKETCHBOOK, available on Amazon.

Other Books From Smith Beach Press

AN EASTERN SHORE SKETCHBOOK: 60+ YEARS VISITING VIRGINIA'S PARADISE

HTTPS://TINYURL.COM/Y77FXBCF

AN EASTERN SHORE SKETCHBOOK is a loving look at the lower Eastern Shore of Virginia. For those who live there or have visited there, you'll recognize many of the people and places. For those who have not, I hope you will be able to read the SKETCHBOOK, find amusement and enjoyment in its reflections, and perhaps transfer some of that to memories deeply seated in your minds of your special place. So much has changed on the Eastern Shore over the years. And yet everything remains the same. That's the beauty of The Eastern Shore, at least the Lower Shore. It is a way of life that has been proven by time and tradition. It shows that you can be surrounded by the manic bustle of modern life, but still remain gentle and genteel. It shows that there can be things more important than a dollar—like history and tradition and manners and civility and friends and a tried and true way of country life. Those of us who look to the Lower Shore as an anchor or normalcy in our frantic rat race lives can only pray that the forces of development (development does not necessarily equal progress) and the quest for the almighty dollar do not ultimately destroy what for now is such a joy.

FREE BOOK

HTTPS://DL.BOOKFUNNEL.COM/OQF4NBI56E

SATAN. ACCORDING TO a 2007 Gallup Poll 70% of Americans believe that Satan, the Devil, is real. Another poll revealed that 42 percent believe people are occasionally possessed by the devil and a full majority, 51 percent, said people can be possessed by the devil or some other evil spirit. "Some other evil spirit." That's called "a demon." Do you wonder where demons come from? EZKEEL IN THE BEGINNING is the prequel to The Demon Series, but it is Biblically-based fiction that will answer that question for you.

SCAM (THE DEMON SERIES BOOK 1)

HTTPS://TINYURL.COM/Y2974RS3

"Americans gave $410 billion to charities in 2017." Giving to international charities was $22.97 billion, 6% of all donations.

—Nonprofits Source, Bethesda, MD

IN THE ABJECT poverty of Haiti all that Daniel wanted was serve his little group of followers, at first in his mountainous home village and later in the slum of Cite Soleil. He didn't seek fame or fortune, only fulfillment. But when his worship unleashes a lwa, or Vodou spirit, he is led to dreams of bigger and better — a church and, later, an orphanage all paid for and supported by donations from American congregations.

What Daniel doesn't know is that his lwa is actually Ezkeel, an ancient fallen angel. Ezkeel tutors him into scamming monies from American churches for the development of his church in Cite Soleil and later subscription-financed orphanages. What his donors don't know is that the church touted to them as an outpost of Christianity in the midst of crushing poverty is actually a Vodou temple, and the many children they are paying monthly subscriptions to support . . . don't exist.

THE EXQUISITE CORPSE (THE DEMON SERIES) (VOLUME 3)

HTTPS://TINYURL.COM/Y9UUL6Q9

NORTHAMPTON COUNTY, LIKE so many rural areas, is still strongly ruled by Bible-believing Christians. One of the benefits of rural life has always been that the corrupting influence of the big city, with its humanists and moral relativism, was far enough removed that it tends not to taint their society. Satan finds it easy to make inroads in metropolitan areas. There, he has the pseudo-intelligentsia to work with and do his labor for him. When convinced of their own excellence and intelligence, people's minds are relatively easy to twist inward and away from a spiritual leader. Really, they do the evil one's work for him. All he has to do was a little poke here, and a little direction there, and they merrily race along in any direction that feeds their egos and avarice, and leave a judgmental God far behind. It isn't as easy in rural areas, and that's why Ezkeel and his kind have been sent to work directly and intimately with these folks. His goal is to influence people by directing their minds to abandon their long-held traditions and beliefs — beliefs based on Judeo-Christian teachings — and accept the more liberal New Age beliefs that eschewed an established God who established right and wrong, and instead made everything relative. Ezkeel is an expert at this, having labored in this field for years, and he was having a ball in Eastville. These chumps were so malleable. Whispering suggestions, gently pushing, quietly suggesting and watching them grab the thought and take off with it was a real pleasure.

Made in United States
Orlando, FL
24 April 2023

32402186R10124